ZOMBIE-
NEXUS

Collection 1 *unedited*

By S. Fairbrass.

S. Fairbrass

For Chelsea, you've kept my head up whenever I was down, you were my light in the dark and you filled my life with reason, a feat never accomplished before or since. Although we're not together you still stood by me

Thank you.

Foreword.

It all started with a dream or should I say nightmare, as I sat and dwelled on it the following morning, I realised this could become something bigger.

So, I pulled out my phone and began a skeleton version (A basic structure from points A to B that covers the main idea with as little detail as possible), which eventually evolved into the book you are reading now, I have come up with so many different characters that I was unable to fit them all into just one book.

Looking to authors like George R.R. Martin who famously started the Game of thrones saga and the Kirkman/ Moore partnership that gave us the masterpieces that are the Walking dead Graphic novels, I developed my own stories, using these giants of the era as inspiration.

Initially my book was named Z.N. which at the time stood for the extremely unimaginative Zombie novel, pretty rudimentary right? So, wanting it to sound more captivating I decided to keep the Z.N. acronym and set about coming up with a far more interesting title focusing on words beginning with N. I eventually settled on the word Nexus and the rest is history!

Nexus: to establish a series of links or connection.

When I finally settled on this word I didn't actually know what it stood for I just thought 'Zombie – Nexus,' that sounds cool and more importantly there seemed to be something right about it too.

My main aim from way back in 2014 was when I created all these characters I wanted them to eventually be introduced into some of the stories, throughout the novel, linking their individual stories and merging them into one, which in a way cemented the word Nexus.

As I stated earlier I started with a skeleton story which I accidentally published on Kindle, but instead of taking it down I decided to use it as an experiment, will people like what I have to share? Here's where I'll let you in on a little secret I never even edited it so I wrote it and uploaded it... whoops, but even though the review I got was a measly 2 stars their comment hit me hard but I used it. There was a light in it, they stated my characters were interesting, the just needed to develop! So, even though this version was chaotic and also unprofessional there was something worth pursuing, so I went through it and edited it... and that reviewer was right it was a mess!

Making the entire novel difficult to read was never my intention, I simply wanted to create a story for people to follow and enjoy.

So! After eight years in the making, I finally completed it edited and all, it flows but there are things that just have to be there for the story to work. My intention is to evolve and adapt and become a much better author through my experiences with this book, just know I will never publish an unedited work again.

 Contents

Prologue

As their night came to an end, they found themselves walking along a different route to normal, without the usual rush of the high street it seemed unfamiliar and intimidating.

The sky was clear but the rain from the day before made the ground soft and damp underfoot, small puddles reflected the moon's light in an eerie, ominous way and minutes strands of water had evaporated into the cool night air leaving a fine layer of mist as they trudged on.

The blackened surface of a river reflected silhouettes of themselves back at them, as they aimlessly wondered alongside it, ignoring the copies of themselves that disappeared into its depths.

Darkness was pressing in on the two of them creating a stronger feeling of discomfort. He pulled his arm tighter around her shoulders, allowing her to smell the oddly pleasant mixture of his sweat and cologne, the warmth of his body close to hers was reassuring and welcome.

The wind stirred around them rustling reeds at the river's edge not far behind, they seemed to continue rustling like shambling footsteps long after the wind had died, adding to the unsettling atmosphere that was bearing down on them like some form of predator.

The solemn shadow of a bridge loomed up in front of them, stretching over the winding river and disappearing into the distant fog far beyond the furthest stretches of the river, there were no streetlights to illuminate its frightening profile, making it even more foreboding. The mere sight of it caused her muscles to tense, which forced her to shake uncontrollably, her companion mistook that she was cold, so he removed his jacket and placed it onto her shoulders. It was warm and unnecessary, but she did not reject the gesture.

She had never been here before she felt lost, terrified, still he continued and still she followed, the sense of timid curiosity mixed with the growing fear of being left behind overwhelming her.

The wind blew again this time making the hollow beneath the bridge groan, like voices of many hidden assailants echoing from the black dense opening beneath the giant stone arch.

They pressed on, hearts pounding in their ears. She could feel him stiffening becoming more alert, it made her feel even more unsettled. Another groan from the wind, but their focus lay ahead of them, straining their eyes wide in the darkness, fearing to look back.

She saw it then, an odd shape on the ground just ahead of them, just out of reach of the darkness, illuminated in the pale moonlight.

At first, she thought it was a fallen tree trunk, as they drew nearer the details grew clearer, their eyes focusing more as they approached, slowly with each step it mutated into something far more sinister.

A smell clawed at her nostrils, causing her to gag, it was sickening. She turned away, closing her eyes briefly as she tried to filter clean air through the stagnant cologne sprayed onto the jacket draped over her shoulders; after a while she took a deep breath and managed to force herself to look back at the prone body.

A silent scream formed in her throat, it wasn't a tree, far from it, it was the body of a man, he was sprawled out on his back as if he had fallen from the bridge above.

He appeared to have been dead for a while, the stench was just a clue but the rotting flesh on his face had confirmed it. Sloughs of it had fallen away in places, leaving the bone exposed, his mouth was open in a frozen expression of fear, eyes open and unblinking, glazed and lifeless.

As they stood there taking it all in, thoughts pressed in on her making the fear even more real, were those bite marks? She thought, maybe an animal? but they looked... human?

What had happened? had they stumbled across the scene of a horrific murder? she wanted to persuade him to turn back, to run away, but the words wouldn't form, she had become mute, paralysed by the fear that had consumed her rooting her to the spot.

They hadn't noticed that the wind had stopped, but the groans from the bridge behind them continued despite this. Silence descended upon them briefly as they took in the macabre scene, only to be replaced by more groans, uncertain on what to do next, she clung onto him harder.

He tried to stoop down to investigate further, but she held tighter onto his arm, preventing him 'I'm jus' gunna get a better look' he reassured, like a fool she consented, releasing her grip. He lowered himself into a squatting position looking at the body from all sorts of different angles, grimacing he pulled out his mobile, pressing the number 9 three times, before dialling.

Did she really see what she thought she did? Had the body just moved? Her eyes widened and a scream had left her mouth before she could stifle it, diverting his attention back towards her, this was not what she wanted, she willed him to run, but all she could do was watch helpless; what happened next was the product of some form of nightmare, it couldn't be real, a slow jerking movement at first, then before he could react it was alive, it was pulling at him, biting him and scratching at his body, almost trying to tear him apart piece by piece, all of a sudden its mouth was full of his skin, barely chewing before it lunged in again for another taste.

He collapsed, dying, screaming for her to help him, as the creature descended upon his twitching body, devouring more of him in a frenzy of inhuman hunger, his bloodstained phone discarded to his side, a woman's voice called into the air '999, please state your emergency,' before the screen went blank as the battery died.

Tears welled in her eyes as she started to back away, his voice gurgling as he drowned in his own blood, his movement stopped and he lay motionless, the attacker feasting on him unaware of his companion nearby.

It was all her fault if she hadn't of screamed he would be fine he could still protect her, she had to run, but before she could even turn several pairs arms were around her. Suddenly pain erupted from her neck and arm as she felt what was unmistakably teeth plunge through her soft skin. She fell to her knees and so did they; blood pouring from the fresh wounds, she began to scream, her voice growing weaker, another sharp bite and she could see her life passing into the blackness of nothing in front of her and then... silence.

In the distance a TV played to itself, A news reader called out to an empty room, as the wind carried the sounds of screams from all directions in through the open window, within seconds the world had descended into chaos.

Jack 1

The sun had begun to set beyond the horizon, Jack Connors was perched on the roof of his house, twiddling a large kitchen knife in his hands; he stared blankly wherever the light danced across the tiles at his feet. What he wouldn't do to have a gun, it would be a great solace he thought to himself, but there was little chance of getting one. His Dad used to have one hidden in his drawer amongst his socks, but that was before this had all started, the chances of it still being there now, were slim. The reoccurring thought crossed his mind of the many elaborate methods of obtaining the weapon, he had dreamt about from the beginning, however he shook them out of his head as fast as they entered, as if they were nothing but jokes.

He closed his eyes as the last light from the sun hit his face, it illuminated the dried streaks left by tears on his cheeks, tilting his head back slightly he embraced the delicate heat before it disappeared behind the horizon, causing the temperature to drop dramatically.

Even though the Sun had gone the sky was still bright, the brief beauty of dusk was accompanied by an eerie quietness, it was this that made Jack shiver, not the pressing cold, he glanced into the distance where he could make out the outline of the city, he could see plumes of smoke climbing their way up into the gradually darkening sky, exhaling heavily he paused to think about the earlier events.

He had turned 21 not long ago, in fact it was only two days before the world was turned upside down, he was young and fit, but he was no athlete and spent too much time in his room playing on his games consoles, this resulted in a very poor amount of stamina, but he knew he could run if he had to.

His mother once used to say that he was a looker, with neatly chiselled features and perfectly blue eyes that worked well with the sandy mess of hair that covered his head. He pushed it off his face and thought of his mum and how she was one of the first, he remembered how she hadn't been well for a long time and how his dad had gone to check on her, lying with her to keep her company in her final moments, however he had fallen asleep, it was this mistake that had sealed his fate.

Jack shifted slightly as he sniffed back the tears that had begun to resurface, his Backside was growing numb again, it was difficult to keep balance for so long on the hard roof tiles, yet he had managed it, for what? three hours now? Must be a record he thought, but there was no use for records now, not now the world was gone.

Three days had passed since the first news broadcasts of a new sickness that was claiming the lives of so many and no one had any clue of what was going on, for the most part he had been sat on the roof watching as it all played out before him, the only other place he deemed safe enough to venture was his bedroom which he only returned to for food or water. It was an attic room separated from the rest of the house by a ladder; a ladder which had been hastily pulled up the day his family had turned.

He would, after all be one of them, he pondered if his brother hadn't sacrificed himself to keep Jack safe, he would have become a 'shambler.' A name Jack came up with as it fit perfectly with the way they moved, disjointed, unnatural and aimless.

His stomach churned to signal his return to his room to find something to eat. Shifting his weight forward he gracefully slid down the tiles to the window of his room, which was sticking out of the roof like a trapdoor.

Lowering himself cautiously onto the floor of his bedroom he could hear the gurgling groans of his family below, sniffing back the tears once again he began to scour his room for food. Empty crisp packets filled the bin in the corner and the odd chocolate bar wrapper decorated the floor around it, he had given up caring about being tidy as he kicked over clothing in his search, eventually something caught his eye. Perched on his dresser was an orange, he wrinkled his nose at it looking once more for something else, *anything* else; he never had a taste for fruit, but it was all there was, it would have to do.

He moved towards the dresser and picked it up, looking it over hunting for a reason not to eat it, any trace of mould would do, but other than the fact that it was softer than usual he found none, after all it had only been there for a just few of days.

So he proceeded to start peeling it, wrinkling his nose at the pungent spray of citrus that ripped at his nostrils, freeing the fruit from its waxy skin, he shovelled the segments three at a time into his mouth, he was finished in seconds, it hadn't been as bad as he remembered, but that may have been the circumstances that had caused him to think this, when he was done he carefully crept towards the hole in his floor - the only way to reach the levels below - he lowered himself onto the carpet next to it, dropped the Orange peel through the opening - something he would have never done if his mother was still alive - where it landed with a very little noise, yet it was still met by excited sounding rasping breaths as a lumbering figure came into focus, looking around frantically for the source of the sound.

Very like Jack in looks his brother was Four years older, he was once called Dan, but there was one key detail... Dan was unmistakably dead, no longer in any real need of the name that he once responded to; its head was hanging to one side and where his shoulder met his neck was a large wound, a bite mark, dried blood spilling from it, giving colour to the otherwise grey skin.

Jack shuddered and turned his gaze towards the rest of the room below, it was a horrendous sight, all the furniture had been up ended and there was dried blood everywhere, here and there bloody handprints had decorated the once blue walls, adding a macabre contrast to the grandeur of the once well cared for landing.

The door to his parents' room was off its hinges, lying within the threshold. Jack could only just about make it out as the landing grew darker, he knew that this was where his parents were... when it all started.

His mum had come home from work, only mentioning something about feeling unwell, she went straight to bed without any dinner. Jack knew that this was unlike her, she would usually talk about how her day had gone, normally she would regale them with all sorts of stories about how the senior member of her workforce: Old Jane they had called her, who would somehow lock herself out of the office, when her key card was stilling hanging round her neck, yet somehow caught on the other side of the door.

Yet that night there was no tale of Old Jane and her shenanigans, only an uncertain air filled with worry.

It was *that* night after they all went to bed, the sickness claimed her, while everyone else slept, She Suddenly sat bolt upright turning towards her husband, who was awoken by the sudden movement, preceding to bite a chunk out of his throat before his eyes had adjusted to the scene, the combination of his guttering scream and inhuman growl from their mother woke the boys up. Jack jumped out of bed with a loud 'THUMP,' ready to answer the call, whatever it may be, but it was this that must have caught his mother's attention, as by the time Jack was at the ladder he witnessed her leaving the room. It was her that tore the bedroom door from its hinges, with a strength so unlike her own usual delicate manner. She began hunting for something, anything to quench the hunger that now consumed her.

Dan who had also heard the commotion was in the landing, Jack was on the floor peering blindly into the room below through still blurry eyes, blindly he watched it all unfold.

Mum lunged in Dan's direction in bloodlust, but he was ready, ducking out of her way she went hurtling into the bathroom, promptly Dan as if trained for such an occasion, seized the old bookcase propped up against a nearby wall, sending its contents spilling out in all directions, he used the shelving to barricade the door, 'DAN!' Jack called out in warning but by the time he had turned around he was face to face with their reanimated father.

Wound at his throat dripping tremendously, clothes stained with blood glistening in the dull light. The two of them began to struggle, something fell to the floor, but Jack was unable to make out what it was and watched helplessly as his Dad's strength overpowered his brother's and managed to take the chunk out of Dan's neck, Dan pushed out with the last of his energy and their Dad fell through the banister, tumbling down the stairs, Jack heard but did not see his head smashing open on the door handle at the bottom, rendering him once again lifeless.

Dan looked up to Jack, an expression of pain on his face, 'Pull the ladder up,' he groaned and Jack did as he was told, knowing that he too would eventually become what their parents had, by the time Jack had returned to the hole stowing the ladder in his room, Dan had clumsily slumped against the wall where the bookshelf once stood and slid down to the floor, letting his blood pool around him, staining his clothes and the carpet, looking at his older Brother, Jack could see tears forming in his fading eyes Dan whispered through the pain now consuming him 'Jack... I love you... keep... yourself safe... and don't... hesitate... to end me... when-.' Jack watched as the life left his brothers eyes and his body went limp before he could finish his sentence, then shortly after barely even minutes passed when there was a faint rasp of breath that signalled his reanimation.

Sleep had become very difficult from that night on and the dreams didn't help, re-enacting the events that had taken his family away from him, so quickly and here he was staring down once more at what had become of his brother.

Dan shambled off Jack could hear him knocking things over somewhere else on the landing and pulled himself away from the hole, he made way across his room and climbed into bed shutting eyes tight, trying to block out the noises of the Shamblers below.

Before he knew it, he was dreaming of more ways to obtain his dad's gun, one after another, it was only the last one forced his eyes to snap open, it just might work!

He could see light making its way through the window as the sun had begun to rise again, with it, the strangely familiar scent of decay.

Dragging himself carefully out of bed, he crawled back towards the hole, peering down into the landing, he was going to escape today, or die trying.

The used-to-be Dan was still there shuffling aimlessly around in circles, below the hole and he could hear mum banging around in the bathroom, scraping and scratching at the weakening wood of the door.

He had to get down there, but how? If he slid the ladder down that would attract its attention and as he descended, he would certainly be a goner.

Sitting up he glanced around the bedroom trying to find something that he could use to distract the Shambler's attention. He found an empty metal change tin on top of his wardrobe, one of those sealed tins with a coin slot cut into the top and pulling some change out of his jeans pocket, he began to fill the tin with the metal coins, back at his rooms entrance, looking down he saw that Dan had become interested in the clanging tin and was reaching blindly in jack's direction, Jack took a deep breath and flung the container in the direction of the stairs, it flew through the air hitting the wall and dropped out of view, making the perfect amount of noise. The coins clanged around in the container as it bounced off the steps and into the darkness beyond, the excited shambler charged towards it, he too disappeared down the stairs and out of sight.

This was his chance lowering the ladder slowly and carefully he fastened the clips, securing it in place and proceeded down. This is suicide he thought as his bare foot touched the carpet slick with blood, the feeling was enough to cringe, 'wish I'd put my shoes on first,' he muttered as he crept towards his parents' old room.

The sight that met his eyes made him heave, pulling himself together he took in the scene, blood was everywhere even on the ceiling, accompanied by a sadly familiar yet unmistakable smell of death, flies had somehow managed to find their way into the room, buzzing around the bed where e a majority of the death residue had collected, Jack swatted at a couple of them as they flew at him like miniature fighter pilots, an unwelcome greeting.

Forcing himself to ignore them he edged round the bed towards his dad's sock drawer where the gun was usually kept.

It was already open, with his heart in his throat he plunged his hands into it, throwing socks in all directions, but his hands only found bundled up socks and the wooden bottom of the drawer.

His heart sank, where the hell was it? It should be here, then the inevitable thought came to his mind.

'Dad must've had it on him!' he whispered to himself leaping gracefully over the bed, he slid on the slick blood on the floor but maintain balance.

He returned to the landing to the groans of his mother still trying to escape her prison, not noticing the cracks now entwined within the paintwork, as he drew closer to it and luckily, he saw no sign of his brother, He exhaled sharply and headed to the top of the stairs.

Pulling a jagged piece of the banister from under the overturned bookcase by the bathroom door he moved slowly down the staircase, he armed himself and proceeded down further into the unknown.

He could hear noises in the kitchen which must've been Dan as he approached the bottom of the steps, his dad's lifeless torso lay a couple of feet away, holding back the urge to vomit, he begun to check the remains. Hands searching spider-like, his fingers came across the holster nothing more, glancing at the floor around the body still nothing, where was it? 'FUCK!' The word had escaped his mouth before he could even think to stifle it and at a volume he could unfortunately not control.

Dan's gurgling moved closer more excited, he'd been spotted, Jack saw the unmistakable shape in the doorway, glancing down he saw the stock of the gun sticking out of Dan's bloodied pocket.

It must have been what Jack had heard fall to the floor in the struggle and Dan picked it up when he was dying on the floor, Dan raised his arms and moved awkwardly towards his younger brother, gnashing his teeth hungrily.

Eyes closed, Jack swung the shard of the banister around aimlessly, hoping to make contact, but all he could hear was it cascading off the wall and the stairs on either side of him, then finally the sickening 'THUNK' of wood on skin.

His eyes tore open he had managed to knock Dan off his feet, with his brother's last words echoing in his mind, without thinking he brought the banister down on his brother's head, once, twice, on the third swing he felt the wood vibrate firmly as it struck the floor and the gurgling stopped and a single welcome sigh replaced them, as if his brother was set free.

The body still twitched a few times, then nothing, it was lifeless once again coming to rest not far from their father, a wave of relief entwined with sadness rolled over him, as he looked to the body in front of him.

Dropping the piece of wood, his hands flailed frantically and once again holding back the intense urge to vomit, he pulled the gun from his brother's pocket it was dripping with brownish blood. Jack felt his head throb unpleasantly, he had become deaf from the coursing adrenaline pounding through him, so deaf that he did not hear the loud crash of splintering wood from upstairs, as he slumped against the wall next to him catching his breath.

Allison

Less than Twelve hours had passed since the alarms had sounded and the zoo had erupted into a frenzy, though it wasn't animals everyone was trying to escape from, it was those *other* people. Disfigured shapes that now rasping and snarling through the bars separating a small animal enclosure from the main zoo path, that twisted its way through the entire complex, crouched in a corner of this confine were two girls, any animals that once occupied the cage were nowhere to be seen, even if there was a chance they had escaped, their chances of survival beyond the cage that once detained them were slim.

Both girls were in their mid-twenties, Lucy Brathwaite was 6 minutes older than her twin sister Allison, she was energetic and courageous, it was her idea to chance the enclosure to protect themselves, until a better alternative presented itself.

'What if the animals are still in there?' Allison cowered, she was far more diffident than her sister, it was hard to believe they were even sisters at all, except the fact that they were pretty much identical, the only way they you could tell the two apart was that Lucy was slightly skinnier.

Lucy had the door open before she answered, 'I'm sure we'd have better luck with some rabbits than *them*.' she Gestured towards their pursuers, chasing them with the hunger for human flesh, fresh in their eyes.

She pulled her sibling into the cage and slammed the door, with a loud 'CLANG,' moments later the biters were flailing their arms through the bars, trying desperately to get hold of some fresh meat, the girls moved away from the entrance until their backs hit the wall of the noticeably empty enclosure.

More biters had joined since then and Lucy had begun to doubt that the cage door would hold with the current onslaught of bodies grappling through the bars, the bars were starting to shake and would be soon free of their supports and the biters were trying harder to get through.

One of them had even managed to get its head though the bars leaving the rest of its body from the shoulders down safely outside the enclosure, as it now flailed one armed on the floor, snarling at the girls, skin hanging off its face where it had been torn away by the rusting poles.

Lucy ran her fingers through her short blonde hair, in frustration she stood up, exhaling sharply and started pacing on the spot. There had to be a way to save themselves from the grim fate so many other had suffered not long before, Allison curled herself up in the corner, she watched her sister move around the enclosure in front of her. Lucy had decided to take it upon herself to find some form of way out, staying as far away from the entrance as possible, yet examining all aspects of the housing that enclosed them, growing frustrated at the lack of help she was receiving, 'ALLI! Stop whimpering and help me find a way out of here!' she shouted at her sister, before looking around the pen once again, her green eyes darting here and there, for anything of use.

Allison watched as her sister began to move some rocks about searching, then she moved her own attention elsewhere, looking around and taking in their surroundings, trying her hardest to ignore their spectators that were reaching so desperately towards them, their features disgusted her; she noticed their confinement was set out similarly to the monkey house but on a much smaller scale, there were little wooden platforms built into the trees and plastic ropes interweaved between them, she turned her attention about the rest of the chamber for anything that could help better their chances of survival, it wasn't long when she saw it halfway up a wall, a ventilation grate, behind that would be a shaft! Slightly obscured by Ivy clinging to the section of wall above.

'Luce there's a vent up there,' she whispered pointing it out to her sister, Lucy followed her sister's finger, clambered up onto a nearby ledge and tore the foliage away from the wall, where it was dropped carelessly to the floor, the faceplate wasn't very big and the opening behind it appeared to be just about wide enough for Lucy to crawl through.

looking up she saw immediately that the mounts had become brittle, maybe brittle enough for her to pull it off, set about trying to remove the grill with a kind of frenzied haste, however the bolts despite their tired appearance remained firmly in place.

Examining it further she saw she may be able to slide some sort of metal pole or even a rope between the faceplate and the wall and ease it off that way, she looked around for something try pry it open, there was nothing she could use within sight except rocks, all the ropes bound to the trees were bolted in place, there was no way she'd be removing those.

The snarls grew more frantic as two more joined the number, making the bars shake harder, this gained Allison's attention, looking towards them she noticed by the cage entrance that there was a loose coil of rope sitting neatly on the floor, however it was too close to the biters for her to risk.

'Luce? Would that rope be strong enough to pull it away?' she asked pointing at it, but not moving to obtain it for her sister, she wasn't going to give them a chance of getting hold of her, she'd seen what they could do and she did not want it.

Lucy moved towards the entrance and tried to grab the rope, as soon as she moved closer the mass struggling through the bars became more active, swiping their limbs in her direction fiercely.

Lucy gasped another had managed to lodge itself between the bars like the first, only this was a small boy around the age of 6, he had made more progress than the other larger biter, both of its arms and a larger portion of his body had wedged through the small gap, the only thing preventing it from getting further into the enclosure was the others carelessly stomping on his lower half, turning its lower half into a macabre fleshy pancake that melded to the concrete beneath; if she hadn't known what it was capable of Lucy would have shown him some pity, but her mind was focused solely on retrieving the loose rope.

The small biter was within reaching distance of the coiled rope pile and Lucy had to be careful, Allison watched as her sister risked her own safety to save them, edging around the room slowly, she had gotten within arm's length of the rope but so too had the little boy, Lucy had to be quick as it reached in her direction snapping its tiny jaw hungrily at her, arms clawing wildly at the air between them in a desperate attempt to fill its endlessly empty stomach.

Stooping down she managed to grab hold of the rope but at the same time the little boy's hand grasped onto her sleeve and began pulling itself closer to her, tearing itself in half, under the weight of its companions.

'GET...OFF...ME!' she yelled kicking out, the heel of her boot made contact with the tiny skull but it refused to let go she kicked again this time at its arm so hard the bone broke, the little boy released his grip, she stumbled away and to the back of the room reuniting with her sister, the tangle of rope clasped firmly in her hand, the young boy's broken and unmoving on the floor its skull caved in where Lucy's foot had made contact, there was no time for pity.

Allison watched as her sister climbed back up to the vent and set about working the rope behind its facing, worming it through a couple of the slats, tying the ends together tightly so she could attempt to pull the vent away, jumping down she tugged the rope, trying her hardest to pull it free, but it only moved slightly.

'ALLI! Help… me!' she demanded as she gave it one last attempt on her own the vent cover again moved slightly yet remained securely fastened to the brickwork.

Allison pulled herself to her feet, reluctantly joining her sister and grasped part of the rope firmly in her hands, they both pulled as hard as they could, the rope slipped a little in her hands she felt the friction of the fibres burn between them.

Eventually with both of their efforts, the metal vent cover gave way with a loud crunching sound, with nothing to hold their weight they both fell to the floor, landing inches away from the struggling biters behind, scrambling up they hastily moved back towards the wall below the vent. without its slated grill blocking their vision they saw a cramped looking ventilation shaft.

Lucy looked at her sister reassuring her 'I won't be long, just wait here!' knowing her sister all too well she hastily added 'don't go anywhere unless the coast is clear,' she didn't want to go, but what choice did she have, it was the only way and there was no chance Allison fit into the vent even if she wanted to.

'Luce... Please don't leave me!' Allison begged but her plea fell upon deaf ears, Lucy had already made up her mind and she was forced to watch as her sister disappeared into the vent.

The biters snarled louder, they'd lost half of their meal, the bars rattled violently making Allison more uneasy, knowing that they'd try harder to stop the other half escaping, lowering herself to a crouching position again, she covered her face with her hands and she began to sob.

She thought back to yesterday when everything was normal, where people didn't eat each other and the dead... The dead just stayed dead.

It was Just another day at the zoo, a trip for their 22nd birthday but no... everything had to be the exact opposite to the way she wanted, it *had* to be ruined, Allison didn't care that people were dying, she only cared about her own well-being, not even Lucy was special enough to receive the same adoration that Allison had reserved for herself.

She was thoroughly enjoying the day, eating a double chocolate ice-cream with Lucy and gawping at the monkeys, pulling faces at them, that one monkey in particular, that had tried to pull a face back through the glass, that separated them from the visitors, this in particular had added an extra air of improvised perfection to her afternoon.

With a huge smile on her face, she pulled Lucy over to the Lion enclosure, where a huge male Lion was patrolling the nearest edge, almost strutting as if he was showing of its prowess, when suddenly alarms blared into action from all around them, she knew that sound, it was the emergency siren that meant a dangerous animal had escaped? but how? More importantly... why today?

She overheard an obnoxious sounding teenager calling loudly to her friends '*I* bet some lazy ass security guard has gone and fallen asleep on one of the buttons, it's just a false alarm.'

There were other frightened rumours from strangers rushing past mentioning something about needing to get to the panic zones, high above the animal enclosures.

They decided not to risk it and followed the panicked crowd in search for a safe place, they were not far from the stairwell when her focus was diverted, a large group of people were running towards them from their right, there movements were strange, as if they were limping, like their limbs were not functioning properly.

Allison could not believe what she was seeing, she saw what appeared to be blood spatters decorating their attire, she was certain she could see that among the crowd was a person with one arm blood spattering from an exposed artery and another with their intestines spilling out onto the floor, but surely she was imagining this no one could be up and moving in that sort of condition, could they? The crowd was moving far too quickly for her to confirm this.

Within moments these strange people had caught up with the group the sisters had merged themselves into, now Allison could not only see the stained clothes, but the bite marks on cold dead skin shining with more blood, seconds later she saw them attacking and biting other people, razor sharp teeth stained red sinking deep into other people's skin, pulling large portions away, she could hear the deafening screams as they fell and she continued to watch as they began feasting on their fallen victims.

The girls turned quickly on the spot, running in the other direction, holding hands, they hurtled past screaming mothers cradling dying children in their arms, the cries of anguish cut short as more of the creatures turned on them, Allison was thinking solely of one thing, herself! As she always had, releasing Lucy's hand, she pushed her way in front of her.

They discovered the cage not far away from where they were.

Now here she was alone watching as further biters became tangled amongst the mess at the bars, that were now shaking even more violently, she watched as people who had lay dead seconds before, returned to life with a fresh unquenchable thirst for blood and a hunger for flesh, joined the fray reaching through the bars, trying so hard to devour her, she drew her knees in tighter towards her chest, and began to rock on the spot, the old residents were still nowhere to be seen but paintings on the wall told her it was lemurs that once resided here, a plastic sign was hanging from the bars, it spun as the biters pulled and pushed at the bars ferociously, eventually it came to stop briefly, just long enough that she could read what it said.

Lemurs,
Temporarily relocated,

Now found next door
To the twilight zone!

The sign relieved her slightly as it meant she would receive no unexpected surprises, from inside her prison, but she now realised how they must have felt locked away with odd creatures staring back at her, she looked back up at the dead taking in their individual appearances, some of the mothers and children they had watched run down the day before were among them, groaning and clawing at her, she also saw the unmistakable uniform of the friendly zoo worker who had sold them the ice-creams they had been enjoying before the day was ruined, his name tag dangling loosely from his torn shirt read 'Terrance.'

The lights around the enclosure flickered slightly, and she shifted closer to the wall again, the biters were making too much noise for her to hear one of the upper supports break, but she saw it, as the iron door began to bend under the weight of the biters pressed against it, she began to shake it was going to be a matter of seconds before the whole thing collapsed allowing her unwanted audience, backstage access, she began to sob again, heart pounding in her throat 'LUCY! WHATEVER YOU'RE DOING, HURRY UP!' she screamed through the waves of hysterical tears 'LUCY!'.

Almost as though in response a Loud siren erupted outside to the right of her cage, the biters that were fighting to get to her had turned in the direction of the new sound, many deciding to head towards it, giving up their futile attempt for a snack, in due course leaving only three struggling shapes, that had managed to lodge themselves between the bars, who were now fighting to pull themselves free to follow the rest, the bars had gotten dangerously loose now, the racket outside had stopped and was replaced by another loud siren only this one sounded further away, for a moment she celebrated but her attention was reclaimed by the sound of the second support breaking her heart plummeted when the bars finally gave way.

'L-LUCY!'

Collings

'Red Bravo to Blue Alpha do you read me...? Blue alpha come in... What's your 20...? I repeat... What's your 20...? over...' SPC Collings repeated himself a third time, but he was only answered by a gentle hiss of static from the HAM radio's amplifier.

At 28 Collings still looked young for his age but after months stationed in Syria he had aged a lot mentally even if it didn't show on the surface, tattooed on his cheek was a long thin scar which represented precisely how close he had once been to death; his eyes a steely grey, working with the short dirty blonde hair the screamed of the appearance of a haunted past.

'Still no response Serge,' he called to a square jawed man stood on the back of a nearby Jeep, A large Red letter 'B' stencilled on its profile, it had been almost a whole day since the Blue

Alpha team were sent to investigate the town up ahead and they hadn't checked in since announcing their arrival at the outskirts, which was now nearly 20 hours ago.

It wasn't like them to breach protocol by going so long without logging a response, or even giving their location, after all they were professionals, their training dictated that they provide regular updates whenever possible, even if they were pinned down.

Collings could scarcely believe the reports they had been sent to investigate, the dead were coming back to *life?* No, it couldn't be true, just how could it? It was just like the movies they used to release when he was younger, yet here they were with no film crew in sight.

He'd been a fully qualified Specialist in the military for nearly two months now and was top of his platoon, heck he could even be Sergeant one day, well so they said. But like the others he couldn't help but feel scared, if they returned once, what's to stop them returning again?

'Double tap to the head' were the only orders they had been given, *easier said than done* he thought.

They started as a group of sixteen of the finest operatives in their regiment and eight of them had gone ahead into silence. A couple of creepers had made their way towards them, Collings thought for a second that they may have been returning soldiers, but as they drew nearer he could see that there was no sign of any form of military attire.

It was sickening sight, with their faces skin decaying, so colourless and inert, slowly a sickening aroma swept over them like a wave of poisonous gas, it was horrendous, a pungent mix of sweet-smelling perfume and week-old rotting meat, even from a distance the smell was so strong you could taste it in the air.

As they had been instructed they fired silenced bullets through the skulls two at a time and they collapsed where they were, to a more permanent grave.

'Another hour and we're going in after them,' the Sergeant called once the firing ceased at the fall of the last creeper, Collings relayed his message a fourth time and yet again, he was answered by static silence.

As the hour passed into nothingness, several more creepers made their way towards them and Collings continued to spam his message, still the speaker echoed no response, just a gentle whisper of the wind swirled around them, when suddenly out of nowhere a woman's voice groaned out of the radio.

'Red Bravo, this is Blue Alpha... Do you copy...? over.' Collings grabbed the mic hastily and pulled it towards him spouting a new reply.

'Red Bravo, this is Blue Alpha... Reading you loud and clear... What is your 20...? over...' He called into it, once again for a short while there was nothing but silence again, the voice seeming as though it was a ghost on the line.

'Red Bravo...urgently requesting backup...O-' Came the reply, it was cut short, replaced immediately by a cry of anguish followed by a gurgling sound, like someone drowning, then the static returned swallowing the responder's final moments.

The eight Soldiers looked at each other with terrified looks on their faces, the silence broken again by the Sergeant's powerful voice, 'Collings, you, Corporal Hendry and private Gale, we need you to scout the location out,' he spat, 'the rest of us will be right behind you, Scramble Privates!' he finished with a roar.

'What, only the three of us Serge?' responded Private Gale, a was a very nervous character and the youngest in the squad, he was very small and agile, but when it came to stealth there was no competition, his muddy brown eyes stared through a mess of hair of almost the same colour, the patchy stubble across his chin only highlighted his youthfulness.

'Yes, Private we need as many men as possible in case more of those abominations come! the three of you will be able to slip by unnoticed,' the Sergeant hissed impatiently.

Reluctantly the three of them set off on foot, leaving the other soldiers to pack the gear rapidly into their two remaining jeeps, parked at the edge of the makeshift camp.

'Right, we need to double check our ammo make sure we got enough,' Collings gestured to his belt where he had multiple magazines of varying sizes, he had about five for his handgun and another nine for his MK-5 assault rifle, along-side these he had a machete and a small blade, just in case.

The other two had near enough the same, however Hendry had managed to misplace his handgun, back at the base so the other two divided his ammo between them.

The wind picked up as they approached a badly weathered sign large white letters etched across its green surface there was blood spattered across it making it impossible to read, not that it *really* mattered anymore anyway, they passed it without a second glance.

Pulling on their gas masks, they pressed further into the town, shooting down some more of the creepers, along the way, they kicked in doors to nothing, but macabre scenes of death, ransacked shops, abandoned houses or disturbing more creepers, barely giving them the time to take in the intruder's presence before they were vanquished.

This was proving more difficult than they had thought, when they saw the overturned frame of what was unmistakably a military jeep the large blue letter 'A.' sprayed onto its side, told them it was a Blue Alpha vehicle.

Not a good sign Collings thought, as they approached, neither was the sight of one of the soldiers pinned underneath it, dead, a large portion his face had been eaten away leaving his skull exposed in places, blood spattered the tarmac around him, his left arm had been severed and lay several feet away, that too have evidence of cannibalistic feeding.

The body twitched suddenly and slowly its eyes opened beneath the mess of flesh around them, clouded as though blind, but it caught sight of the three soldiers standing over him and began to snarl, clawing aggressively at them with its one arm, gnashing its teeth,

Hendry stooped down stabbing his fallen comrade in the skull with his blade, putting him out of his misery, resting once more.

The others had to be nearby, turning to the others Collings communicated silently with his hands telling Gale – the lighter footed of the three – to move on ahead to scout the surrounding buildings, while they waited for the rest of their team to arrive.

The young Private consented unwillingly and disappeared behind the jeep, leaving just the Two of them looking back along the route they had just travelled down, the road was clear as far as they could see, there was nothing except a few burnt-out wrecks of cars and several bodies that were scattered among them.

A noise to their right caused them to raise their weapons ready from more creepers, instead a panting Gale emerged from beyond the overturned Jeep's bonnet pushing his back against the metal roof, his face white with horror and struggling to speak through fear.

'G-g-guys I-I think I-I found them,' he stammered breathlessly, clutching a stitch on his side.

'What's got you tongue kid?' Hendry's voice was gruff and biting but there was an underlying edge of warmth this time, he always had a light heart, in the current circumstances it was a welcome trait.

Gale said nothing and just gestured for them to follow.

After rounding two corners, they saw what had terrified him so, there were hundreds of creepers, indulging themselves on the remains of three of the Blue Alpha team, the other four soldiers, still unaccounted for.

They crept round the side of the nearest house, peering carefully around the back-edge Collings made out more creepers fighting to get into the back door of another house two buildings down, there must be someone inside, they had to check it out.

There were too many of the Creepers to take out without being discovered, there had to be another way, surveying the area he saw a small metal shed in the garden next door, it was anchored to a small section of the side wall of their target property and just above it was a large open window, the gap in between was small enough for them to climb.

Climbing over the low wire fence they made their way across the garden and onto a pile of wood conveniently stacked up next to the shed, they pulled themselves up one at a time, Gale went first followed by Collings, who was then tailed by Hendry, once on the roof they clambered up and in through the open window, as Hendry pushed off of the shed roof, it collapsed with a resounding crash, drawing the attention of several creepers; leaning out of the window the soldiers watched as they arrived at the scene in a frenzy of disappointment, turning away, looking around sheepishly forgetting what they had been pursuing moments prior, they stumbled away in different directions.

They found themselves in a bathroom, the door was barricaded with a wooden chair, the only source of light was from the window behind, which left the room quite dark, looking around the room they saw a shape slumped in the bath, when they moved closer they saw that it was the Captain, he was still breathing, but bleeding heavily from a wound to his abdomen.

Collings moved over to him cautiously handgun at the ready, but there was no need the captain was still alive, but barely, each breath seemed painful and each exhale escaped like a stutter.

'Captain Flint? Can you hear me?' Collings called to him, the captain groaned and nodded weakly signalling his response, his voice lost in the agony on his face.

His mask was dislodged and around his neck, the others took off theirs, breathing in the fresh air. 'Captain where is the rest of your squad?' Collings knew the answer before it came.

Flint mouthed the word Dead, his eyes barely open, unable to focus he winced and with a slow rasping breath he passed out.

Suddenly they heard a frail pounding on the other side of the door, signalling the arrival of a creeper, they were trapped.

 Brad

The streets were wroth with activity as the whole city evolved into a frenzy, the citizens had begun pillaging all the stores for anything they could get their hands on, TVs, Stereos, even the sweet shop had its share of raiders.

Brad was in his early Thirties and had been arrested more times than he could count, mainly for stealing, but there were no cops about and he just really wanted a new car, something expensive, a large Lamborghini garage lay just out of town with enough choices not to pass up and even more perfect, it was abandoned.

So, here he was crowbar in hand, Wearing a recently acquired Ralph Lauren hoodie that was grey in colour and obviously stolen owing to the security tag still clasped to its hood; strolling between the luxury sports cars on the forecourt, so many to choose from, black ones, yellow ones and even a strangely pleasant shade of green, but no, it was the orange Gallardo that he wanted. He tested the handle, only to discover that it was locked, *no worries* he thought, just need to find the keys inside the office, he didn't want to smash the window of his new beauty.

Swinging the Crowbar from hand to hand he moved closer to the glass building, smashing a window in one hit, it was so satisfying to hear silence, no alarms, a car thief's bliss.

The lights were out, but Brad knew where to look, a small office was located at the back of the showroom and he knew a large key safe hung halfway up the wall behind the desk, he'd been here before.

He started to move towards the door when a strange smell brought him to a stop, confused he stood still sniffing the air curiously, he'd never smelt anything like it, it was an unpleasant concoction of scents like gone off meat and sour milk, he didn't like it, choking slightly and he moved forward once more, he paused again, he could hear something, a groan and a shuffling of feet, someone else was here.

Raising the crowbar in defence he edged closer to the noise, he drew level with a door, the door stood wide open he pressed his back to the thin wall next to it, straining his ears in order to listen, he found that the sound was coming from within.

The smell was stronger here, a strong metallic smell had merged its way into the others, making him feel sick, the noises began to make him feel a sight unease, a strange snapping had started as if warning him not to move any closer.

He stopped, peering through the slit between hinged side of the door and its frame, that was when he saw the what had been making the noises, it was human-like in shape though he could see rotting flesh barely covering bone where it had begun peeling away in places, he stumbled backwards in shock, knocking over a rack full of aerosols and car fresheners, sending them clanging to the floor, as soon as the racket settled, Brad noticed the snarling had stopped and he looked up in time to see the creature appear from beyond the door, it was turning towards him.

'Aww hell no,' he shouted as it bolted across the showroom inhumanly fast in his direction, flailing its limbs in an avid frenzy baring its teeth as it approached.

Brad raised his crowbar again bringing it down hard on the side of the creature's skull, he heard the bone crack and could feel it give slightly through the cold metal bar, the creature was stunned falling towards a wall, recovering it charged once more at Brad only hunger in its empty eyes, pulling the bar up again mechanically Brad slashed at it once more carving his attackers head in two with the edge of his blunt weapon, the thing stopped becoming limp, it dropped to the floor, twitching.

Sweating a little Brad brought the crowbar down five more times until the convulsing had stopped.

He straightened himself up, adjusting the hood that had made its way over his face as he hammered down at the things skull, breathing hard looking at his handy work, sprawled out on the floor in front of him, a sense of triumph on his face Brad saw that it was the shop's owner, a man he had many encounters with in the past.

'Finally got one over on you, this time,' he taunted, the amount of times he had tried to get one of the cars, only to be foiled by the man who now lay at his feet.

Raising the crowbar, he examined the end, it dripped with the same green, brown sludge-like residue, that was currently oozing from the mess on the floor, wiping it in the tatters of the old managers clothes, wrinkling his nose as he did so, he resumed his search for the Gallardo's keys, he reached the locked office door and jimmied it open, the room was empty and he could see the safe on the far wall.

Prying the small metal door was easy, he allowed it to swing open, where it clattered against the wall, now, finding the right key, however there were hundreds of them, but he only had one set in mind, he could picture the orange car perfectly in his mind and soon it would be his.

Scouring from the bottom to the top, he began discarding so many keys with delicate thuds of the carpeted office floor, *this is taking too long* he thought, thumbing through the identical looking keys, each set was labelled, telling him what models and the years of production.

Finally! The right keys at the top of the safe almost the last pair too, grabbing them he spun round and started to jog back to the car, using the remote function to unlock the doors, he climbed in and thrust them into ignition, as he turned them, he let out a whoop of excitement as the car's V10 engine roared into life, such a rush, pushing the image of the creature out of his mind with a single rev of the engine, he slammed the door unwinding the windows as he did.

He drove the car delicately out of the parking lot and pushing his foot towards the floor went hurtling down the street, without fastening his seat belt.

He drove past many of the creatures similar to the one he had just slew, what the hell were they? He wondered, he had never seen anything like it, a few had begun to give chase, but he effortlessly left them in the dust and within seconds they were just small dots in the distance.

He looked out the window gazing at the houses, wind blowing through his hair, shoving an audio jack into his phone, blaring his music on full blast, attracting the attention of more of the shambling creatures as he passed, he looked at the speedometer and saw he was doing well over 100mph.

'WAAHAHOO!!' he screamed excitedly.

He slowed down allowing himself to stare again out of the window, he noticed someone perched on the roof of a house, just sat there not moving, 'what the hell is *he* doing? such a *freak!*' He muttered to himself.

When he returned his attention to the road, it was too late, 'OH SHIT!' he yelled and with a desperate attempt to prevent the inevitable, he slammed both his feet clumsily on the brake, turning the wheel sharply to the left, the car engine stalled as it collided with a police car, skidding then rolling, eventually it came to a standstill on its roof at the side of the road, music still blaring like an ice-cream van, enticing the nearby creatures to a nice quick snack.

Finding himself face down on the roof, luckily, he hadn't broken any bones, but the glass had shattered and had buried itself in his skin, 'well that was *stupid*!' he groaned, forcing himself onto his back.

Pain coursed through him, dull and bearable, as if he'd recently been beaten up, reaching upwards he brushed aside the activated airbag and yanked his phone out of the audio jack, hushing the booming music, its screen was smashed to smithereens, angrily he tossed it out the fragmented windshield, where hit something making it snarl furiously, several of the creatures had begun to bear down on the wreck and he could see their feet approaching slowly.

'Karma's a bitch!' he joked, embracing what he thought would be his final moments, as the melted hand reached in towards him, he fainted.

Jack II

A numbness surged through Jack's entire body, did he really just put an end to his brother? He knew Dan was already dead but did he really have to do *this?* A thick dark mud like puddle of blood was now oozing out of Brother's opened head onto the floor, tears once again started to form in Jack's eyes.

The shock had started to fade when a creaking noise caused him to look up, about halfway up the stairs, a foot had appeared, his heart sank, no he couldn't do the same to his mother, the woman who taught him so much and cared for him all of his life, until now at least, now she wanted him for a whole different reason.

Stumbling down the last steps came the hunched form of his mother swaying on the spot, her skin pale, dried blood dribbled down her chin and spattered onto her nightgown and her eyes had lost any sense of love that they once had, to be replaced by a cannibalistic hunger for her youngest son's flesh.

Raising her arms, snapping her teeth together, head lolled to one side she charged at him, Jack dodged to his right into the living room and watched as she stumbled into the kitchen, rasping and snarling angrily.

Jack knew what he had to do, but how in the world would he be able to bring himself to do it? He knew that all that was left was a shadow of what she used to be, an empty shell, but it still looked like her, it still resembled his own mother.

She staggered into the doorway of the front room, dragging her feet lazily beneath her, Jack's hand grasped the stock of his father's old gun, taking the safety off, he cocked it, ensuring the chamber was loaded, raising it he preceded to aim it at her heart, using the sights just like his dad had once taught him.

One shot, the barrel kicked back, but the bullet found its target, yet it had no effect, his mother stumbled drunkenly backwards, but remained on her feet, *what was going on?* Were they blanks? No Dad would never use blanks, perhaps it was a miss-fire or dud, he cocked it again and took aim once more, this time firing two shots, refreshing the chamber quickly before firing the second, he heard them both hit flesh but to no avail, she would fall back before shuffling towards him again.

Then he remembered how his brother stopped moving when he hit him across his head and took aim at his mother's, 'Click!' *What now?* Cocking it again only this time no casing leapt out, he had spent the remainder of the magazine and now he was cornered, there was no escape.

His plan had spiralled in the complete opposite direction to how he had pictured it, instead of being back in his room with the gun and both his mother and brother rasping away downstairs, he now faced an inevitable death, either him or this shambling echo of his own mother, *most likely the former,* pocketing the gun he seized blindly at the air behind him keeping his eyes fixed on the Shambler, his hands scrambling around spider-like for something anything.

He stepped back and his left hand collided with something thin, something *metal!* grasping whatever it was and glancing rapidly down towards it he saw that he was now holding the fire poker, pulling at it he found himself subconsciously swinging it round in front of him, pointing it at his mother like a rapier.

Closing his eyes as he had when confronted with the shambling equivalent of his older brother, he thrust it forwards catching something on the point, only the shoulder pushing her back before withdrawing it he raised to about eye level and without even moving it, the shambler pressed forward and the poker pieced its eye, there was no screaming like a real human would, no she simply pushed forward, *harder*, He had to put all his weight behind it to keep her at bay.

When he shot forward a foot or two as the poker broke the bone at the back of his mother's eye socket with a sickening pop, the body went limp and collapsed to the floor taking Jack and the poker with it.

He pushed himself up and brushed down his filthy clothing, he sat down on the sofa to his right and sobbed into his hands, in three days he had lost his whole family, twice! he was alone.

Another thought entered his mind, what would he do now? He wanted to go, leave this place, leave the memories of everything past and present behind, he just had to go, he gave himself some time to relax before he set about emptying all the cupboards of as much food as he could.

He piled as much as he could into the boot of his car, which was sat on the drive, in front of the house. He managed to find ten boxes of ammo for the gun, after searching the boot of his dad's car.

Siphoning the oil from both of his parent's cars into three canisters, he placed these carefully in the footwell behind the passenger seat of his own, a Vauxhall Corsa.

Eventually he was sat in the driving seat of his car and turned the key, the engine rumbled into life and he sat there, the gun on his lap now fully loaded, two more magazines were sitting comfortably in his pocket, he stared at it remembering all those movies of exactly this happening, replaying over and over in his head, it would be so easy to just place the nozzle beneath his chin a put an end to all this hurt, but instead placing the safety on he slipped the gun into the glove compartment below the steering wheel and alternating the pedals, he drove away from the only place he ever called home, the home he never wanted to come across again.

He had been driving for about half an hour when he noticed about five Shamblers fighting to break into an overturned orange Lamborghini, was someone in there? More importantly were they *alive?*

Retrieving his gun from the glove compartment, he pulled up and got out, looking around him, but the Shamblers were the only forms of life anywhere near the orange wreck.

It had obviously hit one of the empty police cars lined up across the road, in some form of roadblock the front end was in tatters, turning his attention to the struggling mass he saw that unfortunately three of the five Shamblers were once police officers, their uniforms torn and stained by their own blood, raising his gun, he fired three shots two found the backs of two of the Shamblers skulls, the third missed, the gun blast drew the attention of the remaining three.

They were on him in an instant faster than his brother and mum, showing they must have turned not long ago, his eyes widened in shock, he backed away firing another shot, managing to take another down, two more to go, another shot another miss, another shot, another down, squeezing the trigger a fourth time 'Click!' *Not again!*

The last shambler was one of the police officers, it was so close now, it was almost upon him then he remembered the kitchen knife, he had strapped it to his belt pulling it out, as it grabbed him, he managed to bury it into the side of the officer's skull, the handle broke off cutting deeply into Jack's hand.

The rasping officer stopped dead once more its eyes rolled upward into its skull as it fell to the tarmac with a sickening crunch, as it landed the knife pushed further into its head, a bulge appeared when the tip had broken through the skull but not the skin, Jack felt a squeamish fuzz wash over him and hastily turned away.

his hand was now red with blood, but he felt no pain strangely he felt fine, his body was surging with adrenaline for the third time that day numbing anything including any feelings he may have felt of ending yet another... life? Stumbling towards the overturned car, he dropped to the floor to see inside, there was a man on the roof of the car unconscious, reaching in Jack checked his pulse, there was a heartbeat, he was still alive, he had to get him out.

Looking around there was nothing around him except the bodies of the fallen Shamblers, the police cars and his own, he had some water in his car, which should bring him round.

He sprinted back to his own car -which stood idling beyond the police cruisers - and returned seconds later with a bottle of water, splashing it on the man's face, who awoke with a splutter. but thankfully he came around, the man looked at what had just splashed him bewildered.

'*What?! How?! Where the hell did you come from kid?*' The man spluttered as water dripped down his face, Jack was about to reply, when from behind came the unmistakeable sound of a rifle cocking a bullet loading itself into the barrel ready.

Alan

The Holiday Park was still as the sun rose, over the tall trees on the eastern side, bathing the sloping lawns in warm light, an old man drew back the curtains of his mobile home, welcoming the sunlight as it filtered in through the window, onto his face.

Alan Crawley was retired, he and his wife Elizabeth were on a much-needed holiday just in time for her birthday.

For the most part, they had been enjoying themselves it was a trip of a lifetime, but it would soon become one they would remember for all the wrong reasons.

They were both about to sit for breakfast, Alan had started frying some bacon and sausages on the small gas burner oven, pouring his wife a mug of tea, which he placed onto a coaster, on the dining table in front of her, followed swiftly by a full English breakfast onto the placemat next to it.

Alan was now seventy-four and his wife Elizabeth was turning seventy-two tomorrow, he had put together a nice surprise for her like he did every year and she was looking forward to it as usual.

Plating up his own breakfast and pouring himself a strong black coffee he sat down opposite Elizabeth, who was waiting patiently for him to do so, before she began her own meal.

Moments later while he was washing up the plates he gazed out of the window in front of him, two men appeared to be arguing outside the caravan next door, it looked as though it was about to get very aggressive, something that rarely happened here and it was becoming so vicious that Alan turned to lock the door.

'Lizzie, I think something's wrong,' he called over his shoulder, his wife had gone to change out her bedclothes and was soon by his side peering out the window as one of the men fell to the floor, but it wasn't over the other man had dropped down too, trying to rouse the other for a second round, or so they thought, when he all of a sudden he lowered his head and tore a chunk of skin from the other man's throat, with his teeth.

Elizabeth's scream left her before Alan could even realise what he was doing, he had his hand over her mouth, stifling her with a veiny hand.

'Get in the front we're getting outta here,' he shouted, fear building in every syllable, never in his seventy-four years had he seen anything like it, cannibals? *Here?*

With a grace and elegance not commonly found in someone his age he had moved the length of the motor home and jumped into the driver's seat next to his wife.

A turn of the keys and the caravan shuddered into life, lurching forward violently it stalled in his panic, he urged 'his little beauty,' to start again for a second time it choked back to life and they were off, listening as they heard muffled screams all over the campsite.

They were gone before anyone else had realised, haring down the park's winding entrance lane they saw more people were attacking each other, but they noticed the victims after they had fallen had started rising again blood drenching their apparel, and their movements were strange, sort of stiff and fragmented.

After a while they were on the open road, with no idea where there were going, when Elizabeth spoke finally breaking the silence that roared between them 'It's a good thing you packed our hunting gear Al,' her voice shook somewhat with terror, noticing this Alan placed his hand on her's to console her.

He had and never would he need it more, people were eating each other! The thought made the hairs on his neck stand on end, and he could feel the Goosebumps pushing at them making them more prominent.

A barren stretch of road lay out before them when the engine gave out, it was completely vacant except for the Caravan, Alan went out to inspect, knowing all too well what it might be.

Lifting the hatch on the front he saw the problem immediately, one of the pipes had burst leaking water over the engine causing it to steam, this had happened too frequently recently and he had brought a few spares just in case a situation like this would arise, after nothing was going to spoil Liz's birthday this year! Well, the caravan wouldn't at least.

Calling to his wife she passed them through an open window along with the tools he asked for, after about thirty minutes, he had shut the hatch and they were moving again.

It was an uneventful journey until they entered a small town, when they saw many abandoned vehicles packed down the street and amongst them, things were moving, slow shuffling movements, to their horror they could see bodies of the dead strewn here and there, as they watched some of these bodies had begun to animate similar to the ones back at the campsite and before they knew it they were shuffling around as if nothing ever happened, joining the others like lost sheep wandering aimlessly between the graveyard of cars.

Slamming the gears into reverse Alan turned the caravan around to find another route.

Within minutes they were back out on the main streets, they ploughed on for another hour or so, occasionally passing another risen corpse or another body torn to shreds.

It was only when they saw the police cars had they stopped again, demanding that Elizabeth remained in the vehicle he stepped out to investigate, arming himself with his hunting rifle, he crept out in time to see something dart across towards an overturned orange car, five bodies were strewn across the road, three were dressed in the standard issue police uniform, by the looks of them they had resurrected like all the others but only to be shot down again.

He saw that one of the police officers was very close and, on the tarmac, next to him was the handle of what appeared to be a large kitchen knife.

Ignoring this he moved slowly forward gun raised he looked towards the overturned vehicle.

A young lad was trying frantically to get into the orange car, Alan's heart stopped the poor lad can't have been too much older than twenty, he was still scrambling around by the overturned car when Alan cocked the rifle.

But when he boy turned to face him slowly, his face was young and full of life, not at all like the other no sign of the pallid complexion.

'Whoa! whoa! whoa! DON'T SHOOT! DON'T SHOOT!' the boy yelled, backing away with his hands raised, one was stained red with blood, from a gaping wound across his palm.

'What the devil are doing boy?' Alan responded his voice low and calm rifle still raised.

'There's someone trapped in there,' He pointed at the car, Alan peered down to look and saw the bloodied man lying there, face dripping with water, Alan recognised him instantly, the short brown hair and goofy apologetic smile was unmistakable it was his Son, Brad.

'Well... well... well shoulda known it'd be you... let me guess cars stolen? Bet the jacket is too...' there was venom in the fatherly voice the tone disapproving and disappointed, Alan's eyes found the tag secured to the jackets hood and shook his head, Brad choosing to remain innocent as possible simply grinned the same goofy smile.

With the young boy's help, they managed to pull him free, other than a few scrapes, bruises and a possible broken hand he was fine.

Brad Brushed himself down apologising and stating he saw an opportunity why *not* take it?

Alan raised a sole hand to silence the onslaught of apologies waving it off like an impatient fly, he instead turned to look at the young lad, who stood by looking slightly awkward, then his attention moved to the bodies that lay around them, 'What happened here?'

The young boy explained how he had come across the wrecked car, how it was swarming with the now dead 'Shamblers' he had called them, and how it was him that had taken them out, both Brad and Alan listened intently.

When the boy had finished, Alan asked 'I hope you don't mind me asking... But what's your name young man?' Curiosity had gotten the better of him, but he wanted to thank the young lad for all he'd done but wanted to at least know his name first.

'Jack,' the boy replied.

'Well, Jack, my name is Alan, this is Brad my son and in the camper over there is my wife Elizabeth but she prefers Liz or lizzie,' he chuckled as he gestured towards his caravan, 'I wanted thank you for your help we are extremely grateful, but I must ask do you have any clue what's going on?'

Jack shook his head and replied tears burning in his eyes 'no I don't but it's taken my whole family,' his voice cracked and he fell silent.

'Oh... I'm sorry to hear that,' Alan said reassuringly, a thought crossed his mind, 'I think the best course of action would be to stay in a group, safety in numbers they say.'

'Yeah did you *wanna* tag along with us only Dad's old camper doesn't have seatbelts and I'll in need of a ride,' Brad spoke in a light voice, but he could not hide the dulcet tones of fear within it 'And well I, err I've kinda totalled *mine*,' he finished.

Jack agreed 'Will we be heading anywhere in particular?' he asked, he didn't think about it till now but he had no idea where it was he was heading in the first place.

'Not too sure myself, best to get far away from here, somewhere much safer, but our direction should be anywhere but the city, seems the denser the building the worse the situation,' Alan announced 'firstly we need to get that hand of yours checked,' he continued 'before it gets infected, Liz used to be a nurse, she should be able to fix it up, in no time.'

'How on earth did you manage this?' Liz asked as she patched up Jack's hand moments later, Jack explained how the knife had broken when he stabbed the policeman, when he was finished he looked at the kind old lady's face, fearing a disapproving look, but instead she returned a look that told him she had understood, 'That appears to be how the world is... unfortunately going to work for now,' she concluded with a sympathetic smile.

By the time they set off again they were driving towards the sunset Alan and his wife, drove in front while the other two followed in Jack's small car.

It wasn't long before they were in the streets of another town where even more of the dead were lurking, they drove through as quietly as possible so they would draw no attention from the hungry hoards, eventually as the night sky darkened above them, they pulled up next to an old shack on the outskirts of a small village, it wasn't much, but it would have to do for the night.

Checking the premises Brad and Jack had deemed the coast clear and they went inside, it was very small two roomed hunting cabin, with two separate beds one double in one room and a single in the other, in the corner was a sofa, Jack offered to take the latter of the three allowing the family to have the other beds, however after arguing it was the least he could do after Jack had saved his life, Brad had manged to persuade him to take the single bed.

The night was eerily silent and still, Alan barely slept, the thoughts of the previous day still fresh in his mind, sometime around Three in the morning he was woken by a gentle scratching at the cabin's front door.

Lucy

'Be quiet!' Lucy cursed in a hushed whisper as her legs clunked on the metal base of the ventilation shaft it was too loud for her liking, she cast her mind back to her sister hoping to God she was ok, those bars had been pretty loose when she had left.

She came across a grill in the shaft peering through she could see the monstrous outlines squatting around their latest kill, a poor Capybara by what she could see of it, *the poor bugger* she thought, turning her head away she continued to crawl through the metal corridor.

She came across another grill peering through this one she noticed it wasn't an animal cell it was an office and judging by the monitors covering one of the walls it was the security office.

Perfect! kicking at the grill, there was a snarl and a gnashing of teeth from beneath her, and suddenly one of the hideous creatures loomed into view. Once the security guard a large a bite mark on its wrist showing how he had come to the fate of his new existence, speckled blood decorated the uniform it was wearing, it look up in the direction of the vent stupidly, it was clear it couldn't see what had made the noise. Lucy didn't know what to do she was too high up for it but she needed to get into this room if she was to have any chance of rescuing her sister.

   She kicked out at the grill harder the second time and to her surprise it flew off - *these screws mustn't have had the same attention as the ones in the enclosure* she thought – it soared through the air in a descending arc, knocking the creature off its feet, allowing enough time to jump down onto a filing cabinet, where she quickly looked around for something to defend herself with, on the desk the other side of the room was a gun it was her only chance, pushing herself off of the cabinet she darted across the room, her hand was on the stock before the creature was even back on his feet, wheeling around she fired three shots, the first hit its leg the other two entered the skull as the gun recoiled.

It collapsed silent, still, dead, unsure of what she had done she stood there for a moment as blood began to seep from the guard's wounds, would it be classed as murder? *Three shots may have been overkill* She thought, she was defending herself; the guard had probably killed someone else at some point, if not her, uncertain the guard would come around again or not she edged around the lifeless form.

Her breath was heavy as she thought about the consequences of her actions, but she shook them away this was no longer the world she had grown to know, things like this didn't matter, did they?

Her attention was caught suddenly by something on the monitors, one of the screens was pointing from within an enclosure, underneath the screen were the words small animals, she could see almost thirty biters pressing themselves against the bars of the enclosure and there sure enough huddled in the corner was Allison her sister, cowering as usual.

She had to do something, cause a distraction somehow, several of biters had managed to lodge themselves between the bars, there was no chance they were going to free themselves in any way.

Looking around the control panel placing the gun on the desk that front the monitors, she noticed there were multiple alarm buttons; one for each of the enclosures, she pressed the one for the Water Mammal enclosure, the alarm erupted out of the loudspeakers somewhere outside as well as in the office she saw a red LED light up beneath the Water Mammal screen, she watched as the entrance to the cage her sister was hiding in cleared. The biters curious as to what the sound was, lumbering off in the direction of the new sound, leaving only the few caught up in the bars embrace flailing helplessly as they tried to follow the others.

She was about to leave the office when she noticed the map pinned to the wall next to the door; examining it she realised that the only route from here to the small animal enclosure was past the Water mammal exhibit, through the dead.

That would not be possible if it was full of shuffling biters and she certainly did not want to chance the vent again, she looked at the map for the next alarm she should press, studying it carefully she saw the bird sanctuary was the other side of the office, looking at the screen for the water mammal enclosure she waited until most of the biters loomed into view switched off the first alarm causing them to stumbled around looking upwards confused as to where the sound had gone. As the began to disperse she hammered down the one for the bird sanctuary, again sirens blared and the red LED under the bird screen illuminated, blinking like a light on a Christmas tree.

Realising that she may not get out safely with the biters so close, she turned back to the map, for further study, - on the screen behind her the bars to the small animal enclosure gave way. - deciding to go for the alarm on the lion enclosure which would allow her to get to Allison and in turn draw them far enough away that they could both get away from the zoo completely. She switched off the bird alarm and pressed the lion one, watching as the biters now headed in that direction.

She turned to focus her attention back to the small animal screen when the sirens stopped and the blaring screens faded before shining black, an ominous sign - she could have sworn she had witnessed the cage door had given Way at last, - the power had gone out, heart racing she pulled the door open, making sure she picked up the handgun, she tore out of the security room back towards where her sister would be waiting for her.

As she drew nearer she noticed that the bars had indeed fallen, fear forced her hairs on end, she started to run faster, trying to clear all negative thoughts out of her mind, she had gotten there to find the cage empty, her sister was gone. The biters that had lodged themselves through the bars had all been crushed by the bar's weight, they lay there still unmoving, an unspeakable liquid flowed from their skulls.

Lucy dropped to her knees and buried her face in her hands tears pouring out of her eyes, she felt the hands on her before she could react, expecting a bite into her flesh she braced herself to welcome it, it never came, her sister pulled her into a hug and her heartbeat slowed down gradually, opening her eyes to look at her, both of them unaware of the thing crawling on the floor towards them. Teeth disappeared into Allison's ankle and she howled out in agony, kicking out her skin tearing away as she did.

Heart back in her throat, Lucy drew the gun and fired at it without aiming, the bullet hit where its legs would be instead it hit entrails that spilled out of its torso, it took another chunk out of Allison's leg making her collapse.

Before she could fire another shot it had lunged for Allison's throat unlike Lucy's shot it hadn't missed, tearing more than a mouthful away, Lucy began shooting a flurry of bullets towards its skull, blinding tears flowing from her eyes, it dropped limply onto her twin's body, pushing it aside she dropped to her knees and pulled her sister closer to her.

Allison's breathing had become ragged, as she raised her arm to Lucy's face, it dropped before it even got halfway and her breathing stopped in one final whispering breath that echoed through the pain that now ripped Lucy's heart wide open.

'Ali? *Ali*? Please... wake up,' Lucy checked her wrist for a pulse, there was none 'NO! ALI? *ALI?*' she shook her sister's lifeless body trying hard to wake her, *she's only sleeping* she thought, more tears blinding her sight and the truth.

She Rest her head on Ali's chest, still holding her hand she cried the hardest she'd ever remembered crying.

For the longest time she just knelt there holding her sister, when a faint rasping noise made her look up, wiping her eyes on her sleeve she looked ahead expecting to see another of those horrid things, no, the ragged breathing was coming from her sister's mouth 'A-Ali?' she asked, her sister eyes begun to open, pale and grey spheres searching for something to satisfy its new-born hunger for flesh.

Collings II

The scratching intensified as Collings set about addressing Flint's wound, pulling his first aid kit out of a side pocket of his pack he turned back to the injured captain, Flint's breathing had deteriorated since their arrival and he could barely stay conscious more than ten seconds before he succumbed to the pain and passed out again.

Collings pulled up Flint's military camo and recoiled in horror the captain was missing a huge chunk from his stomach, how he was still alive Collings had no idea, pulling himself back together he examined the wound again, there were multiple serrations in the skin that looked like bite marks and the wound had a foul rotting scent about it.

Flint slumped down slightly letting out a long sigh, his eyes were open again, but he just stared blankly across the room, death consuming him in an all too final way, pulling the camo back down Collings checked his pulse, nothing.

He let out an exasperated groan and pushing himself away in frustration, the best chance they had to find out what had happened to the Blue Alpha team had now faded into an eternal sleep. He turned to the other two both of whom were bracing the door to stop the rasping creeper getting inside to them.

'He's dead?' Gale asked, his voice wrought with the strain of forcing the closed as his shoulder bounced off the door, the creeper on the other side growing increasing more aggressive.

Collings nodded, gazing towards the window he saw a bird fly by, it was an all too beautiful day almost as if nothing was wrong and everything was perfect, yet everything he had witnessed had proven the opposite.

'Collings!' He heard Gale shriek and before he even knew what was happening there were arms upon him, the once Dead Captain had lunged towards him in bloodlust, grappling with the creeper, he began to grope for his pistol in its holster, but it wasn't there it had fallen out and was now lying about a foot away to his right.

He was pinned to the bathroom tiles with one arm fending off Flint's snapping jaws, the other began scrambling around for the gun, the other two had tried to help out but as soon as any pressure was removed from the door, the creepers outside took advantage and pressed through the door, forcing them to remain helpless where they were.

This was a fight for Collings alone, spider like his hand crawled along the tiles of the bathroom floor to his right searching for the stock of his weapon, whilst the other pressed the flailing creature away from his face.

His hand found what it was hunting for and instinctively directed itself towards Flint's skull, squeezing the trigger as it drew level.

The creeper was ready for it as the gun shouted its attack, it was knocked aside by one of its flailing arms, sending the bullet elsewhere, where it went Collings had no clue, his focus lay on his attacker, readjusting his grip, he aimed again this time when the barrel exploded it was met by silence and the steady trickle of blood falling on his uniform.

Pushing the lifeless body off of him he pulled himself up and turned to look at the other two only, he only saw Gale and to his horror he saw Hendry sprawled on the floor, blood seeping from a wound to his temple where the stray bullet had hit.

Gale was still relentlessly trying to keep the door shut but there were two creepers forcing their way in his attempts were futile and with all the strength he could muster Gale pushed himself away drawing his Pistol, the door splintered and one of the creatures tripped into the room.

They were both once Blue Alpha team their gas masks still secured to their faces, so no chance of them biting the two soldiers inside, though that didn't mean they weren't still dangerous. Firing his pistol Collings stifled the one on the floor, before it even got a chance to pull itself to its feet.

Steadying his aim at the second, as it drew further into the room he could see the fixed expression on its face, and he could see the rasping snarls echoing behind the mask clasped onto its face, through the condensation the moist breathed has misted against the clear plastic mask, he could see a hole in the glass on the mask and wondered whether it was the air that killed him, it couldn't have been, he was breathing just fine without his mask filtering the air around him before he sucked it in.

As it moved closer he took in the death soldier, slowly moving towards him, he took in every detail as a bullet penetrated its skull sending a blackening splatter of blood out of both sides as it entered and left within seconds, grey eyes rolled back almost in relief.

The figure fell to its left as though the bullet had pulled at it when it left the skull sending a blackening splatter of blood from both sides of the soldier's skull as it entered and exited lodging itself into the tiles of the bathroom wall.

'Collings!,' he snapped back to his senses at the mention of his name 'Seriously what's up with you!?' Gale's voice brought him crashing back to reality 'You froze! That's not like you... not at all.'

He look toward Gale noticing the paleness to the private's face, worry apparent in the expression on his features, 'I dunno I felt we were done for... I guess,' he looked at the bodies around him and counted three more to the total of the deceased. If his calculations were right the fate of seven out of the eight Blue Alpha Squad members had become clear but where was the eighth?

They didn't have to look long, leaving the bathroom, they scouted the house like they had done so many times before, during the drills that seemed to have been many lifetimes ago, simulating war games, capturing war criminals and completing raids, one would enter the room while the other would prepare to cover for outside.

As they moved into what seemed to be the living room they wished they hadn't, something had clearly torn the remaining soldier into many pieces in a frenzy and the only recognisable fragments of their body they could make out was an arm hanging from the sofa in the corner the other hand clasped to the receiver for the H.A.M radio in another.

Their mission was accomplished they had found Blue Alpha team after all, now all they had to do was contact the rest of their team.

Collings approached the radio signalling for Gale to cover him, Gale Complied taking up a position by the rooms doorway and Collings tested the frequency, it was working.

He pried the cold dead fingers off of the receiver with great difficulty as rigor mortis had set into each of the fingers, he dropped it to the floor where it landed with a delicate *'Flump!'* he held the mic to his mouth and clicked the button.

'Specialist Collings to Sergeant Phillips... Do you read me? Over,' he called in to it, he echoed himself as was protocol.

It took a while before a response issued in 'Collings this is sergeant Philips reading you loud and clear!' it exclaimed 'Do you have a visual on Blue Alpha? Over.'
He hesitated before responding his eyes fell upon the hand on the floor next to him, as he chewed on

exactly how he should relay the following message: 'Blue Alpha has been terminated Sarge,' his voice felt too casual, hating it he shut his eyes as he bit the tip of his tongue, but this was how they had to relay conversations over the radio, '... and we lost Corporal Hendry...over.'

'What? How is that possible? Over' Sarge's voice sounded shocked and Collings first thought was of how he had broken protocol, I was justified after all Hendry was one of their best men, even if a little bit forgettable.

'Overcome by a creeper Sarge, over.' it wasn't strictly true but he couldn't say he shot him could he? he glanced up at Gale as if to quiet him from shouting the truth but his look was met by an empty room.

Dropping the receiver, and arming himself with his gun, he walked in the hall Gale wasn't there either, where had he got to? There was no sign of him anywhere.

'Collings what's you 20? I repeat what's you 20? over,' Sarge's voice echoed to the empty room behind him, ignoring it Collings moved from room to room looking for his Comrade. Was it possible they still were not alone? Had Gale been attacked? No, he would have heard some sort of commotion wouldn't he?

He turned out of the kitchen, a door stood half open at the end of the hall, as he approached he could see that it led down to a cellar, nudging it open with his foot he gazed down into blackness, he paused for a moment had he just heard a baby crying? No, he must be imagining it, without hesitation he descended into it letting it consume him in its dark depths.

Alan II

The old man dragged himself slowly off the bed feeling the ache of tiredness in his joints, without disturbing his wife Elizabeth, or his other two companions, he proceeded slowly and cautiously towards the cabin door, where the scratching noise was coming from.

He was about a foot away when a floorboard creaked underneath him and the scratching stopped to be replaced by the unmistakeable whimper of a dog, relaxing slightly Alan unlatched the door and opened it enough to let a rather large shape, about waist height dash through.

Closing the door not anything else the opportunity to follow, setting the latch with a loud but reassuring click! He heard Brad stir in his sleep, but only his snores resumed filling the otherwise mute cabin.

The old man turned toward their new guest, it was a young German shepherd, it was cowering in a corner, as Alan took a step forward, it backed further into the corner only to meet the wall where it began Shaking, its tail between its hind legs.

'It's okay... I won't hurt you,' Alan reassured holding his hand out, the dog started to sniff the air and began to hesitantly move towards the Hunched form of the old man, bowing and bobbing its head cautiously as it approached.

They were about a foot apart when the dog stopped still sniffing the air, Alan took a step forward, but this time the dog stayed where it was bowing its head slightly peering upward at him.

Alan bent down to the dog's level reaching out and scratched it behind the ears, he could tell it was a sire – a male – he took note of the dark blue collar, lowering his hand beneath the dogs chin he examined it.

On one side it bore the name "Shep." 'Ahh So that's your name Shep... It suits you,' he said turning the tag in his hand, the other side had a phone number on it, but the power had gone out so he couldn't contact them by phone, if they were even still alive that was, a large wet tongue lashed at his ear, chuckling he scratched Shep absently behind the ears again and let him lick his hand before returning slowly to his feet.

His joints still aching with tiredness protested against the movement, signalling him to go back to bed glancing at his watch which told him it was only 3:15, he whispered to his new companion 'well it's been a long day best get some sleep... Whaddya say?' the dog seemed to understand him as it trotted off towards the fireplace next to Alan and Lizzie's bed, circled on the rug a few times before collapsing upon it, resting his head on his paws, his tail wrapped tightly around them protectively.

Alan could see his new companion's eyes glowing as Shep watched him walk round to his side of the bed and lie down, the moment his head hit the pillow he was asleep.

His dreams took him back to the campsite, only this time Shep, Jack and Brad were there too, they watched through the windows as the men outside had their strange carnivorous fight, except instead of locking the door as zipping off out of the campsite they flung the door open in order to aid the fallen man.

Only he found that the man on the floor was *Brad!* And he was being devoured by a rotting police officer with the handle of a kitchen knife hanging from the side of his head, the Police officer turned to him and lunged toward him knocking him over, it lunged once more this time toward his neck.

'RUFF!'

A loud Bark saved him from his dream's grisly fate, along with a sharp jab to the ribs, Lizzie had poked him holding her finger to her lips, Shep was cowering in the same corner, but an unfamiliar noise called from beyond the door, a rasping snarling sound unlike any he had ever heard before but it was loud like a chorus of voices not one but many it seemed far off but not far enough for his liking.

Pulling himself again slowly out of bed curiosity urged him towards the window to the right of the door, brushing aside the curtain just enough to peer through, the sight that met him made his blood run cold.

Thirty or more Shambling shapes were lurching against the sunrise, about twenty feet away, none of them seemed fussed over the hut they were hiding in, which relaxed him yet they were moving ever so slowly it was a wonder whether they'd get the chance to escape to their vehicles.

He moved back away from the window wishing that they hadn't left the hunting rifle in their caravan, their only solace was the pistol that Jack had and Brad's Crowbar.

Moving slowly into the centre of the room he tapped his leg and Shep trotted towards him allowing Alan to scratch behind his ears.

He admired the confused look on his wife's face and whispered, 'showed up in the night,' to answer it, Shep stopped and sat down looking at Lizzie with his head to one side assessing whether she was a threat, but obviously thought she was not as he approached the frail old lady and began licking her fingers.

The noises outside sounded a bit more distant when Brad and Jack entered the room 'did I hear a dog bark?' Jack murmured groggily whilst rubbing his eyes, his hair was stood on end signalling a good night's sleep, then lowering his hands his eyes fell on Shep at the side of the bed 'where'd this little guy come from?' he asked confused yet slightly excited, kneeling down trying to coax the pupils towards him slapping both arms on his thighs 'Come here boy,' Shep cautiously approached but again couldn't resist the new opportunity for attention, and dropped to the floor and rolled over allowing Jack access to scratch his tummy.

Alan told them about earlier that night and about the horde of the living dead passing by seconds before.

Brad's expression dropped and he rushed over to the window to see if the coast was now clear.

The group decided to look around the inside of the hut for the first time that morning and discovered that it was a hunting lodge, with many stuffed animal heads lining the walls, there were things like deer, bears, and foxes and even what looked like a moose they were obviously trophies from a different country as Alan was certain they didn't live anywhere near here, in fact he advised that they weren't even native to the country.

There was a mantlepiece that adorned the fireplace, many photos perched on top of it dark wooden shelf, the occupants of their frames were mainly all the same mostly the shown a burly red haired man or a beautiful woman with astonishingly long black hair, they were either posing with a kill, aiming a rifle of laying a trap of some kind, but in the centre of them all there was one with both the red haired man, the black haired woman and a young boy, who had inherited his father's fiery red mane of hair and his mother's stunningly green eyes, if they could hazard a guess he was no older than eleven, sat on the young boys

S Fairbrass

lap, however was a German shepherd puppy with a dark blue collar.

'Is this your family Shep?' Jack asked lowering the photo so the dog could see it better, sniffing the dog wagged his tail in response, taking this as a yes Jack pocketed the picture 'just in case you need to remember them,' he whispered giving the dog a subtle wink.

The best discovery was the cabinet full of hunting gear, there were large knives bear traps and even a silenced rifle, they bore a thin layer of dust but were still in good order.

After grabbing all they could they decided it was time to get moving, Alan opened the door to the fresh air unlike the day before there was no sign of rain and not a cloud in sight such a beautiful day.

Stepping out they began to load the vehicles with the hunting gear when a noise caught their attention they turned to look at the thin wall of trees immediately behind them where the noise had come from, when a figure lurched out right behind Elizabeth, knocking her to the ground.

 Aaron |

The night air had turned cold and so did his treehouse he'd been playing hide and seek for what seemed like forever when the screaming had started in the street and everyone started acting strange, getting into their cars and driving away only to end up slamming into trees and other obstructions in a blind panic, if they had made it to them in the first place.

Aaron Klennford would've come out of his hiding place if it hadn't been for the scary man that had attacked the woman next door, he remembered the blood pouring from the gaping wound left in her arm as the man pulled his teeth away, along with a large amount of flesh.

He had only turned twelve a month ago and as a surprise his dad had built this treehouse, now the treehouse was the only thing keeping him safe, there was no way out unless he ran, he knew he was fast but he had no idea where he would run to, he knew about the woods that led towards his dads old cabin but there were monsters in the woods he was sure of it, he had heard them coo menacingly whenever he approached to explore, telling him not to enter.

He looked towards the woods which he could see out of the hole that was to be a window and stared at the space between full of people who were drenched in blood, once dead but now clearly not, it didn't look far but Aaron know he would stand no chance.

He studied the people further their movements Jerky and inhuman, unsettling though Aaron had seen creatures like it in the games his mother had banned him from playing. They were called Zimboes or *something* like that, he never really had a chance to play it long enough to remember the name.

Wish mum would let me play them he thought to himself as he watched yet another pedestrian try to get to their car only to be brought down by at least 4 Zimboes, hungry for fresh meat, their screams cut short to be replaced by noises of guttural disposition.

He was terrified but was sure if he had completed resident evil revelations he would know *exactly* what he could do.

All he had learnt was that flashlights drew their attention and when you have their attention you either ran or you let the Zimboe devour you, as your character tried feebly to fend them off, as he watched he saw that the survivor had failed to do her blood painting the road surface as her fateful ender reached deeper within her open body.

His mind went back towards the babysitter who was still looking for him in the house, Jacqui was her name and he loved it when she looked after him, she didn't know but he loved her, more than see knew.

Looking out the window towards his house he could see the French window, the curtains were drawn and he could see the light streaming out from beneath them.

The garden that stretched between here and there was empty and the gate was closed so he decided to chance it, climbing down onto his lawn he headed towards the glass door, he went to pull it open when he heard it, a rasping noise to his right, he turned in that direction expecting to come face to face with a Zimboe, only to notice that the noise was coming from the open dining-room window.

Sneaking quietly towards it he peered over the sill, he almost screamed there was blood everywhere and there she was, shambling about like the others, he could see Jacqui's intestines spilling out of her stomach hanging there like some grotesque silly string, her beautiful face mutated into a petrified look of abstract horror, as she lay there propped against the wall where she had met her end.

Aaron watched as the new life entered her fragile frame and she pulled herself from the floor ambling off into another room, he noticed as he watched in timid horror She wasn't alone, Aaron could see the front door stood open and other creatures had flooded into the house, shuffling around stupidly.

As he pulled himself away from the window he turned back to his tree house and climbed back up at least he would be safe here at least until morning.

He pulled a large blanket from the chest built into the wooden floor and wrapped it around himself, shivering not because he was cold, he was terrified, he shut his eyes attempting to capture sleep, but there were too many sounds floating to him on the air, making it extremely difficult.

He heard the old monsters in the forest calling to him faintly in the distance, only this time they sounded difficult they were no longer calling out in warning the were calling to him, to tell him that they would protect him, he just needed to come to them.

He didn't remember anything after that when suddenly 'CRASH!' A loud noise forced his eyes open, it was still dark and he had no idea what time it was. Peering back out of the window he noticed the streetlights had gone out and the street was swallowed by the pressing darkness of night, he saw what had made the loud noise and it unsettled him further a large SUV had crashed into the corner of his house and taken the fence out leaving him partially exposed. He recognised the vehicle it was his dad's, the one they had left in the night before, had the come back to get him? The car's lights were shining bright, bright enough that he could see the garden and the road beyond which was bathed in a sinister red of the rear lights.

Yet there seemed to be no Zimboes anywhere inside the light and none in the section of the street now awash in the blood red lights either.

He was going to do it he had to, his parents were going to the cabin so he would find them there, he was going to run for it, his dog Shep would be there too he missed him so much.

He pulled himself out of the tree house onto the lawn over the SUV with its driver keeled over the steering wheel, blood pouring out of a wound in his head. Aaron recognised him as his father, he stopped still and knocked on the glass.

'DAD?!' His voice a whimper 'DAD?! CAN YOU HEAR ME?! ' his dad's lifeless form twitched, Aaron went to open the door and hug him relief flooding through him but there was something odd about his movements were staggered and disjointed like the others, his face vacant and devoid of humanity as it turned towards his son, the warm relief evapourated immediately replaced with the same ice- cold dread, as his father clawed pathetically towards the window that separated them restrained by the seatbelt that ironically had failed to save him.

Tears in his eyes Aaron ran into the woods as fast as his legs would carry him.

He had been running for what seemed like forever the darkness pressing in on him, he would not be afraid he had to get to mum in the cabin.

He slowed to a stop to catch his breath to force the sadness out of him, to stop the tears before the wind burned them bitterly against his cheeks.

A cracking noise forced him to run again blindly tripping and stumbling as his limbs began to ache, the trees began to thin around him and he could see the horizon ahead.

The wind howled past him, roaring voraciously past his ears, he was not alone something had given pursuit but he willed himself not to look, he had to keep running, away into the safety of his mother's outstretched arms, he could see the sun rising ahead of him illuminating two large objects just beyond the line of the trees he forced himself on.

Giving in he Looked over his shoulder beholding his stalker, blood dripping from its mouth and various other wounds littering it's body. A Lone animal hunting down its prey,
He had been looking too long, as he felt himself collide with something, falling with it he braced his body for the worst.

Lucy ||

Lucy threw the ravenous shell of Allison away from her, tears still fresh in her eyes, she couldn't leave her, but sprawled on the floor in front of her was something far from the twin sister she spent every day with, something more deadly.

Slowly with severe difficulty the creature dragged itself up onto its feet, gnashing its teeth, the wound to her ankle forcing a limp every other stumbling step in the direction of its prey.

Lucy wanted to run to leave her sister, escape the same fate, yet she remained rooted to the spot, unable to move, paralysed with grief.

It wasn't just grief that had paralysed her, accompanying it was a wave uncertainty. What would her life *be* without Allison by her side? They did *everything* together, her sister's arm was reaching out in front of her, even in death Allison was too lazy to lift them both, teeth still snapping impatiently as though it was waiting for Lucy to come to *it,* beckoning her petulantly closer.

The pale hand was about an inch away from Lucy's face, hanging limply, when Lucy found that movement had returned to her, instinct had forced the gun she was holding upwards and instinct pulled the trigger; a single bullet span out of the barrel and striking Alison square between the eyes, her head whipped back, blood splattered from the wound in an arc high above her.

The body dropped as if in slow motion first to its knees then forward onto its chest where it lay there unmoving.

Fresh tears reached Lucy's already bitter eyes, as she stared at the blurred form that was once her sister sprawled on the floor in front of her. Blood oozed out of the wounds that the bullet had left in its fatal wake.

Lucy wiped her eyes on the sleeve of her hoody, turning away from her sister's lifeless body, she couldn't bear to look anymore, the gunshot had drawn the attention of the other creatures nearby and so she ran.

She had no idea where she would go or what she would do, *just run* she thought, as far away as possible.

She passed many other victims of the undead, bumping stupidly into walls or devouring a freshly caught victim be it an animal or another human, she even saw many small children shuffling about and joining in with the feeding, she felt pity for them especially barely living their lives only to become mere shells of who they once were.

None of these things took any notice of her as she ran, soon she was leaving the zoo through the empty gift shop which had been ransacked by fleeing customers, leaping over the overturned shelving, she made her way to the glass door and pushed her way through it, stepping out into the car park.

The pandemonium within the zoo had continued outside and immediately she realised there was no chance she was *driving* out of there, the only exit was a mess of tangled metal. Anyone who had managed to get away and escape, clearly tried to frantically force their way out through the gated exit, they had attempted to squeeze themselves through the small ticket barriers at the same time, resulting in a massive pile up of twisted metal and carnage.

Dotted here and there in the wreckage were the unmistakable signs of more dead, feasted upon by more undead, here and there she could see dead and undead alike shut away inside several vehicles trying fruitlessly to escape these confines. There seemed to be no way out, she was trapped.

She stared into her last hoping of getting out of here losing herself in the flames erupting from the wreckage in front of her, a noise brought her spiralling back to her senses.

She twisted round to see what had made such an awful sound, as she did so she saw a small opening in one of the far walls of the car park, and between herself and the hole was the source of the noise.

A male lion was caught in a fierce battle with about twelve biters, it had already struck down three of them but it was slowly becoming overwhelmed by the other nine and more had joined into the ongoing fray, preventing any chance of its escape.

She could only watch as the majestic creature roared once more in its agony and slowly fell to its side allowing its attackers to begin feasting on it, she could hear its fading whimpers, as silents tears slid down her cheek.

She was sad, but this was her only chance whilst they were occupied with their kill, she made her way round the car park staying as far away from the savage creatures as possible, she managed to get to the opening and was about to pull herself through when she looked down.

On the other side of the wall was a steep hill and at the bottom a motorway, it was barren, but she wasn't certain she would be able to make her way down to it without hurting herself, glancing over her shoulder she noticed that a couple of the biters had noticed her and had already detached themselves from the crowd around the lion, moving towards her arms raised awaiting her fall into their clutches. She cast all doubts for her safety aside and squeezed through the tight opening.

As she started down the slope, but too late she realised she was traveling faster than she had anticipated sliding toward the pavement, she was moving far too fast, as her foot met the road surface she felt the bone shatter, she screamed out loudly her voice echoing back from the valley of concrete surrounding her, she clapped her hands over her betraying mouth as she sobbed in agony.

She collapsed in pain, helpless, the final roar of the lion echoing in her mind, knowing it lay on the carpark ground the way beyond that gap in the wall high above her. She noticed she was still clutching the gun in her hand and she dropped at her side with a clatter her mind began to swim as the adrenaline began to fade from her.

The sky started to dissolve creating a mixture of spots and stars that filled her vision, she breathed heavily, trying to move her now useless leg, but the very thought of trying to move it caused the bones to shift, sending a bubble of nausea rising through her, as she tried to fight against it she felt unconsciousness slip away as she fainted.

Collings III

The clunking echo of his footfalls told him that the staircase was made of wood, it was so dark Collings could see nothing, reaching for his torch he retrieved it from the carabiner that attached it to his pack, resuming the covert position he'd adapted previously, resting it atop his pistol he flicked it on, its single beam illuminated the chamber below.

He reached the bottom of the staircase his feet meeting the hard stone floor, he was in a long stone corridor with two rooms one located on either side, the first doorway was on his right it was here that he found what appeared to be a laundry room as he could see rags and other materials hanging from the ceiling and in the corner were two machines that resembled a washer and a dryer, other than that it was empty.

He strained his ears for any sound, nothing, wait... no... there was a murmuring sound, quiet but definitely something, pressing further he noticed that the door on the left was stood ajar and he could hear what sound like breathing coming from the other side, it wasn't ragged like flint's it was calm, warm, alive!

As he approached the breathing grew louder, he pushed his hand against the door allowing it to swing silently, pistol raised ready for an attack, anticipating another of those creatures to come streaking out of the darkness straight for him, but when nothing came he pressed into the room, like a covert operative examining every corner for some sign of life.

When he light moved across a shape in the middle of the room it was Gale, Collings relaxed, he noted that Gale was holding something in his arms, a bundle of rags? Why? Gale rocked them gently to and fro.

Collings assumed he had just pulled them from the laundry room, but when he went to speak

Gale pressed a finger to his lips warning him to stay quiet.

Drawing level with the young private Collings saw that he was holding a small child, who covered in blood, it was fast asleep in his arms, it couldn't have been more than a day old.

'I heard her crying when I was keeping watch.' He whispered, answering the question that was swirling inside Collings' head, 'so I came down here and she was just lying on the floor.'

'Any sign of the parents?' Collings returned.

'That's a negative.' Gale murmured, 'though I did hear something in there.' He finished gesturing to a door at the far end of the room.

'Stay back, keep her safe.' Collings commanded and Gale pulled back to the wall and sat on a rickety chair, cradling the baby in his arms.

Proceeding further into the room Collings could hear a gentle scratching coming from the door, at the base was what appeared to be a large amount of blood, pulling his small hunting knife out ready, he didn't want to wake the child with his gun, he placed his hand on the deadbolt.

Releasing the door with as little sound as possible he allowed it to swing into the room, with a soft creak the child stirred in Gale's arms but remained asleep.

The sound of the scratching was immediately clear, a young woman whose face was as white as snow was lying in the doorway, her white dress stained red by what appeared to be a rather large wound, her breathing was weak but she was still alive.

'Hello, ma'am are you ok?' Collings questioned her as delicately as possible, she responded by meeting his eyes opened her mouth then closing it no sound came out, even the act of simply opening and closing her mouth seemed to take substantial effort.

Collings looked towards her dress, her hand was loosely holding a rag to a spot just above her hip where most of the blood had seeped through the material.

'Can I take a look?' Collings requested and with effort she released her grip on the rag, as it fell away it revealed a deep long gash, reddened and inflamed with corruption, Collings knew immediately what it was she had done 'did you do this? Did you perform your own c-section?' His voice was calm as he looked into the woman's face, her eyes were an astonishing shade of hazel though he could almost see the light fading from them.

She inclined her head the tiniest amount but Collings knew what it meant, looking at the floor around her he saw a short, jagged piece of glass submerged in the blood around her.

Collings shook his head, retracting his hand to his pack to catch his first aid kit, when he pulled it out in front of the woman, she raised her arm palm outstretched and started shaking her head in objection.

'If you want to live, I have to stop the bleeding,' she continued to object a brief fire ignited behind those eyes, Collings insisted 'I *need* to treat you.'

His voice was soft, but it was then that the woman gestured to her hand, using her head as she was too weak to lift her arm.

He hadn't noticed it as he assumed it was just blood from her wound however on closer inspection a bite wound was unmistakably visible, the area around it too smelled of decay, infection had turned her skin black.

'C-can... I-I... see her?' Her voice was Barely audible but he heard it, he gestured to Gale to come over, who reluctantly consented.

When he was next to Collings Gale lowered himself to his knees beside his superior and the woman looked upon the face of her child in his arms.

She raised her hand to touch her face fighting back the tears that were burning in the corners of her eyes, her mouthed twitched but again no sound came from it.

Then she tried again, with a quivering hand still touching her daughter's soft skin 'A-Aurora, ' she whispered with her final breath, her hand dropped to her side and her head lulled backwards, she slumped against the cupboard wall, all live in her body had dissipated.

Collings looked at the lifeless figure in front of him, he wanted to cry and he couldn't understand why, he didn't even know this woman and the countless years of intense training made it difficult to show any emotion, if not impossible.

'Collings... you have to...' Gale paused choosing the words carefully 'you have to... detach... her brain remember, I'll go over here in case Aurora wakes up.' Gale pushed himself up and walked back to the chair as Collings raised his knife.

When he removed it, it was drenched in blood he wiped it on her dress and pushed himself to his feet.

He was halfway across the room when he heard the loud explosions from above rushing out of the room and looking back towards the stairs.

Fire had engulfed the doorway and was burning its way progressively down the stairs leaving no way of escape, the stood at the top was a figure consumed by the red and orange tongues of fire, looking down upon them ominously.

 Abigail !

'DANNI?! JAKE?! COME ON GUYS WHERE THE *HELL* ARE YOU?!' Abigail's voice bounced back of the dense canopy of leaves above her as she yelled for her lost friends.

It was getting late and she was alone. Her husband Tom had gone off to look for their dog as it got spooked by something and bolted, when Tom left he had taken the car with, her friends Danni and Jake had wandered off and left her all by herself, they were probably off somewhere screwing or something, they usually were.

She thought of home and whether Aaron was alright with Jacqui who was looking after him, she was such a good sitter it was a wondering that they ever found someone like her at all, they couldn't trust the other people in their neighbourhood. She then thought of how pink her son's cheeks turned whenever they mentioned

Jacqui, that little smile that crossed his face whenever they said her name.

Aww his first little crush! she thought, allowing herself to smile, when a noise snapped her back to her surroundings, she stiffened alert, listening further a gentle rustle of leaves behind her like footsteps.

She wheeled herself around to see what it was but saw nothing, turning round again she continued to call out for her friends 'DANNI?!' another rustle of leaves but to her left this time 'JAKE?! GUYS THIS ISN'T FUNNY!' the leaves rustled again like someone running, she turned in that direction but still saw nothing, the wind blew, there was definitely movement behind that tree! 'JAKE! IS THAT YOU?!' she approached cautiously, she could hear breathing so she stopped.

'DANNI?! I KNOW THAT'S YOU! DON'T YOU DARE JUMP OUT ON ME!' her voice was uncertain, heart in her throat, when the wind blew harder than normal, a branch poked out from behind the tree, waving as if saying hello.

Her nerves settled and her heart dropped, but as quickly as it had nested it had sprung straight into a heavy rhythm again something had grabbed her around the waist from behind, screaming she spun round and came face to face with Danni.

Her friend was smiling broadly, her make-up smeared, over her round face and her hair was pulled back in a lazy ponytail, as though it had been hastily tied, several twigs, leaves and even a bird feather had entwined themselves in the mess, telling Abi she been lying on the forest floor at some point.

Fear was quickly replaced with annoyance she could have slapped Danni but she stopped herself and instead pulled her friend into an embrace relief spreading through her whole body.

'You could have given me a bloody heart attack!' teeth clenched and jaw set 'Where's Jake?' Abigail questioned, knowing full well he would probably jump out any second now too.

'Oh, Abi seriously you need to lighten up a bit, he's just over there putting his trousers back on,' Danni laughed 'though its so off-putting hearing you call our names out every *five* seconds, puts a weird image in your head when you're... *y'know*, ' she finished with another giggle, pulling her skirt down, neatening it in a tell-tale gesture.

'Well sorry Danni but I haven't heard from Tom in over *two* hours! and I'm a getting a little worried... and to top it all off you guys had vanished for *one* of those hours too,' she looked at her friend hearing her own words and thought how motherly she sounded.

'Oh, sorry Abi, we didn't think about that, ' Danni stuck her bottom lip out almost sounding as though she was mocking Abi, but this was what she did and Abi just rolled her eyes at it, she couldn't stay mad at Danni, after all she and Tom were like that before Aaron came along.

'Just try not to do it again,' she scolded.

'Oh, no promises there, Sis,' adjusting her skirt again with a wink, they both laughed, their laughter was interrupted by a man's voice, yelling, in pain?

'That sounded like Jake,' Danni's face was white she looked terrified, a look Abi thought that didn't suit her, but this was not a time to stand around.

At first she thought it was another prank, but she quickly rejected the thought, neither of her friends' acting was that convincing. She grabbed Danni by the wrist and pulled her towards the shouts if it *was* Jake, he obviously needed help.

'STAY AWAY FROM ME... I'M WARNING YOU...' The shouting grew louder as ran then gradually weaker and almost as if he was struggling with something 'GET... OFF... ME YOU... PSYCH-,' his shouts broke off, replaced by an odd noise that sounded as though he was gargling water, as if he was drowning, there was no water nearby was there?

They approached a clearing and in the middle were two shapes one lying on the grass motionless, the other crouching over it, but its back was to them so they couldn't see what it was doing.

They moved closer and they could see that the shape on the floor was Jake he was bleeding heavily from a wound to his throat.

His trousers were down by his ankles and he looked like he had fallen backwards trying to escape something.

The other shape was a woman, her clothes were torn and she was covered in what looked like blood.

'ALRIGHT, PUT YOUR FUCKING HANDS UP NOW!' screamed Danni, holding her hand together as if she had a gun. Hoping the trick would work but the woman didn't listen, instead her head snapped round inhumanly fast and to their horror her face was dripping with blood, *Jake's* blood, an eyeless socket glared sightlessly in their direction, there was something evil about its stare, her movement was staggered and disjointed, as she moved to her feet.

Staggering to one side revealing a hole torn in Jake's stomach when she rose something fell from her hand, where it hit the earth with a revolting *'Slap!'* across the leaves below, before they could see what it was she was bearing down upon them, her jaw clicking as teeth rose up and down, chewing on something.

Instinct forced them to run, they ran in different directions and the cannibal streaked after Danni.

Abi looked over her shoulder and saw she was alone, stopping herself, she could hear Danni's cries behind her moving further away in the distance.

Turning on the spot, she back in the direction Danni had run two shapes flitted between the trees ahead, her mind made up she chased them, using Danni's yells as a guide.

Jack III

Jack had his dad's old gun out ready, aiming it at what had knocked Lizzie over, but quickly lowered it, the kid was holding his hands in front of his face at the sight of the weapon and was clearly afraid.

'What are ya doing on your own kid?' He whispered but before the boy could answer, the reason he was running became clear, a shambler loomed into view, its face drenched in blood it was snapping and snarling fiercely, limping in their direction.

Jack cocked the gun and raised it taking aim after learning from his last mistake he steadied his aim on the creature's head, he went to squeeze the trigger but his hand was nudged aside by Brad who ran wailing in the direction of the creature his crowbar raised above his head.

With one downward swing the metal shaft made contact with it skull and it dropped out of view, the group watched as Brad made an odd kicking motion before swinging the crowbar down a second time silencing the creature once and for all.

He turned and walked back over to them a grimace on his face, 'Don't wanna be firing off guns in case it draws more of 'em out,' he shouted when he was about a foot away, Jack took note of the fleeting look of pain that flickered across his face, eying him suspiciously he shot back a retort.

'What... more than you wailing and shouting like *that*?!' Jack responded his voice a little gruffer than he intended.

He turned to the kid who had pulled himself up and also helped Elizabeth back to her feet with the help of Alan and was now apologising profusely.

Jack could tell he was on the verge of tears, doing his best to keep them at bay, he moved toward him 'where's you mum n' Dad,' he asked looking the small ginger lad in the eyes, *where have I seen this kid before?* An internal monologue, a question that held no answer.

'They were out with some friends and dad came home, only he...' the boy wiped his eye on the sleeve of his jacket but carried on 'only he crashed and became a Zimboe.' He ended bursting into tears.

Jack heard the word 'Zimboe,' and managed to catch the smirk before it appeared on his face he chose not to correct him, not while the poor kid was so distraught about losing his father.

'Hey buddy don't... its ok... we'll look after you, maybe we may even find you mum.' Alan seemed to know what he was doing as the young boy sniffed a few times and looked bleary eyed at the old man.

Without warning, he flung his arms round Alan's waist 'thank you mister,' he whispered.

He released the old man leaving a snot trail on Alan's cardigan 'so what's your name buddy?' Jack asked trying not to sound too patronising, realising at last where he had seen him before, he pulled the photo out of his pocket, examining it, it was definitely him, no question about it.

'My names Aaron,' he responded wiping his eyes again, 'have you not seen my mum?' He continued 'its just that this is my parents hunting cabin.'

'Oh... no we haven't,' Brad answered watching as Aaron's sniffed miserably again, Jack cast another glare back at Brad, he was holding himself differently, ever since that weird kick, grimacing he looked back at the picture in his hand.

The cabin belonged to the boy's parents it confirmed what Jack was thinking and he moved over to Aaron and held the picture out to him 'I picked this up inside and kept hold of it for some reason I guess this is the reason, maybe it'll help you...' pausing from a moment he thought carefully about what he was about to say next, remember you parents, he couldn't say *that!* 'If you start to miss you parents,' he added Squatting down to Aaron's height he handed the photo to him a reassuring smile, Aaron took it with a watery smile.

'That's when we got Shep, I hope he's ok too! I don't know what I'd do...'

Jack straightened up and walked over to the caravan door, 'Oh I have a feeling Shep's fine,' he tugged at the handle and like a shot the German shepherd bounded out, diving right at Aaron and knocking him to the floor for a second time, laughing this time Aaron reached up and hugged the dog tight, happy tears rolled over the trails left but the sad ones.

'Poor kid,' Brad mumbled behind Jack as he opened the boot of Jack's car dropping his crowbar inside 'well we gunna hit the road or not?' He called as he slammed it back down.

'I guess we could try and make towards the coast see if we can find a ship or something,' Jack had seen it in many films although it always seemed to be a futile attempt but the others seemed to like it.

'There is a port about half hour *that* way,' Alan pointed as he spoke 'the only issue is... that was the way all of them critters went earlier.'

They would have to chance it, they agreed that that was the next course of action and so they set off, Aaron and Shep went with Lizzie and Alan in the caravan and Brad and Jack in the car.

Jack thought it was odd the for the first time since they met that Brad neglected to blast his music and was sat very quietly in the passenger seat. 'Brad... you not gunna play your music?'

'What? Oh... yeah,' He fumbled the button on the console and music come through the car's speakers much quieter than the previous journey.

They drove past hundreds of Shamblers that wandered aimlessly through otherwise abandoned streets, giving chase briefly eventually becoming small blemishes in the car's rear-view mirror.

Jack kept his attention in the road before him they were approaching a valley that was completely free of life, no movement except the caravan in front. To the right was a high man-made wall, every inch of which was adorned with a fantastically beautiful combination of colours, graffitied images of dragons twisting around each other, painted high up on the brickwork.

On the opposite side was a steep grass slope, another wall stood at its crest with another smaller masterpiece plastered upon it at the base of this slope was a lone shape. As he passed he saw it was the body of a woman just left to rot at the side of the road.

He glanced sideways at Brad and noticed that he was extremely pale the cocky grin was gone and sweat was dripping down his face and he seemed to be drifting in and out of consciousness.

'Brad? How long have you been infected?' it all made sense the wincing, the fever, the strange smell and that weird kicking motion, before he swung the crowbar down the second time. Brad only stirred slightly, just shook his head and stared out of the window, but Jack knew he was right he recognised the symptoms, he had seen them before this was exactly like Dan before... Brad was speaking so he listened, he didn't have much time left.

'Think... we... need... to... stop...' he breathed finally after several minutes passed, 'gonna... be... sick...' he ended, Jack pulled the lever at the side of his steering wheel to flash his headlights so Alan could see they needed to stop he clicked it down the caravan pulled up and Jack eased up alongside it.

Brad fumbled gingerly for the clasp of his seatbelt, he seemed lost a destitute so Jack released it for him, Brad managed to pull the door handle himself and flopped out of the car unable to hold himself up, Jack rounded the car and pulling Brad's arm over his shoulder, his breathing was slow and seemed to require a huge amount of effort for Brad to force out.

'That... thing... bit... me...' he whispered as Jack lowered him against the side of his car, Answering Jack's earlier question as if he was experiencing a delay.

With difficulty Brad pulled up his trouser leg which Jack noticed was stained with blood, revealing a small wound, clearly infected, veins of green extruded form the break in the skin, twisting their way up his leg and disappearing below the denim of his raised trouser leg.

'Why didn't you tell us! You could have turned and killed one of us!' Jack didn't know why but he felt angry, he was sad but his frustration was indeed justified as he stared at the man who he had rescued a day ago.

'I... didn't... think...of...that' he spluttered and he turned away to wretch, a small spatter of blood erupted from his mouth spraying the ground with the crimson red fluid.

Alan had joined them, immediately seeing the blood, he had no words just a grave expression of worry etched across his face.

Jack couldn't look at him it troubled him, why did everyone around him seemed to end up dying? He thought he heart heavy was he a jinx?
'Brad you don't look well,' Alan's voice measured and calm, he had seen the bite, swallowing he looked at Jack who could only nod solemnly, 'Oh Gees,' he said the emotion rising in his hands as ran them through his hair in distress, 'How am I going to break this to Lizzie?' he started pacing backwards and forwards cradling his head in his hands.

Jack had no clue what to do he wanted to help, but just watched on in silent vigil, he felt pathetic and useless and deep inside a pounding feeling of shame he believed it was all his fault.

Alan stopped in front of his son and crouched down to his level holding his son's paling hand.

Jack stepped back to give them room to speak 'is there anything you need son?' His voice was calm considering he was very much aware of the inevitable conclusion that was drew ever closer.

Brad just shook his head the effort forced his eyes closed 'just.. leave... me...' the words left his mouth in something less than a whisper and each word was an effort for him to utter.

'Your mother and I are so proud of you son, regardless of some of the questionable decisions you may have made we love you so much,' the old man wiped a tear from his eye with an aging hand.

Brad looked at his father as if to return the sentiment, but words would no long form on his lips he was far too weak now, a single tear left his eye and his skin paled and his body wilted to one side, as the last breath steadily escaped his chest as if he had tried his hardest to hold on to it.

The old man stood up and Jack could see the grief wet on his face, the once jolly smile he wore earlier that morning was replaced by a look of despair, tears streamed down his cheeks disappearing into the whiskery beard that covered his chin.

He looked at Jack and back at his son who lay crumple at the side of the car and mouthed the words 'Thank you.'

Jack still didn't know what he should do they had to continue but they couldn't leave Brad here like this the had to move him or even bury him, another thing Jack knew was that soon he would come back, how would he put Brad down in front of his parents?

Or would Alan be the one to do it? Before he could suggest anything Alan was moving his son's body away from the car considering his age he was very mobile and moved the body with ease.

'We can't leave him here,' Jack's voice was shaking remorse taken its hold on them as they hung in the air 'he'll come back as one of them,' hearing them Alan turned to him his hand out the palm facing up, Jack had no idea what he was asking for.

'Jack... your knife please.' His voice was different, weak, almost a whisper Jack knowing what was about to come consented and placing a small hunting knife he had taken from the cabin into the grieving father's outstretched hand.

Slowly the old man whispered something to his son's lifeless body drawing Brad's head forward to plant a soft fatherly kiss on his brow, he pushed the blade effortlessly through the back of his son's skull, he wipe it down on Brad's shirt as he withdrew it, holding it out handle first, taking it back Jack watched Alan walked away, broken, and hurt he disappeared into the caravan.

A sound drifted on the wind taking Jack's attention he turned sharply to face they had come, not far away was a solitary figure silhouetted against the sunset, limping towards them slowly.

 Collings IV

The figure stood there teetering on the edge, the wooden stairs had weakened as the fire continued to burn the silhouetted it fell forwards, falling through the stairs as they gave way, brittle underneath the weight, it hit the floor of the basement where the concrete was amas with the burning remains of the staircase, the flames dwindling as wood decayed into a mass of black charcoal the embers still glowing with heat.

As this too faded a whitish grey ash remained, Collings approached it the body indistinguishable among the blackened mess that littered where the stairs once stood.

He could feel the heat from the still burning house above but there was no way he and Gale and the little baby could all climb up there without getting burned by the roaring inferno that sustained up high.

Gale appeared at his side holding the bundle of rags that was the baby Aurora, the light dance off his face, highlighting just how young he really was, 'are we trapped?' He whispered his face confirmed the doubt in his voice, but Collings shook his head.

'Houses like these always have some sort of secret exit or another way out,' Collings was sure of it and as he spoke he began scouring the corridor then he was reminded of the laundry room full of rags.

Pushing the door back open he stepped into the space, moving from corner to corner he found no signs of another way out, even as he traced the fingers of one hand across the wall searching for seams, cracks, even a draft that could have been signs of a hidden door pressed into the stone, there was nothing.

With a heavy sigh, he turned back to the door where Gale was stood, something caught his eye, on the floor between them was a metal manhole cover, wide enough for them to fit through.

He positioned himself over it and tapped it with the barrel of his gun, a hollow metallic note sounded from where the gun struck, he set about looking for something to haul the cover up out its circular confine that pressed it flush to the concrete floor.

Looking once again around the room he noticed a clothes prop ironically propped up against the wall next to what resembled an old tumble dryer.

Grabbing it he proceeded to bend one of the ends like a crowbar, just enough to allow it to hook under the heavy metal disc.

Pushing the hooked end through one of the holes, he pushed on the other end with a considerable amount of force, the cover moved slightly, but not enough.

Gesturing to Gale for help, who reluctantly placed the sleeping baby gently into a nearby wash basket and turned to help Collings with the manhole cover.

They both pushed hard on the pole and with effort the disc rose out of the hole and they both forced it round but it dropped back into the hole with a soft thump, the makeshift crowbar bent under their combine weight, they both collapse to the floor.

'We... need to... lift... it from... both... sides,' Gale spoke through heavy breaths as he looked around the room for another prop, there wasn't anything of use left in the room. He moved to the door and disappeared out of the room, Collings could hear him clanging about in the other room.

It was then that the baby started crying, Gale's shadow was on the door but it stood stationary for a moment flickering as though dancing upon the door, quickly it moved into the room followed by his own body, shutting the heavy door behind him fastening the deadbolt as quickly as he had entered.

He braced himself against it awkwardly there were soft thudding noises coming from the hall, behind the now locked door.

'Creepers!' He gasped he was clutching a rusty crowbar in his hand in the other an odd blue hook as he stepped away from the door Collings heard it the same rasping noise that the Blue alpha team had made, when they burst into the bathroom upstairs, an event that seemed almost a lifetime ago.

The baby's cries, like a dinner bell to the creatures as they now slammed against the portal, banging impatiently begging for entry.

Gale handed Collings the blue tool which he guessed was actually the exact tool for the job judging how its tip fit perfectly through the hole in the metal. The two soldiers hastened in their attempt to remove the drain cover, fear not something that they felt often, removing it easily by lifting it from both sides, the adrenaline coursing through their bodies made the job much more effortless, the cover fell with a clatter on the concrete floor.

Several more explosions reverberated around them causing the ceiling to sprinkle them with minute particles of dust, they were moving closer, every so often Collings swore he could hear the familiar pops of far-off gunshots.

Gale picked up some extra rags from around the room cramming them one handed in his pack, he looked at Collings with a shrug 'we may need them,' as he walked to the basket that held the now shrieking child flailing weakly within.

He picked her up trying to calm her as she screamed furiously, standing over the hall he handed the bundle to Collings and lowered himself into the sewer, within moments he was stood at the bottom Collings crouched down beside the opening leaning in he handed the collection back to his companion.

When she was safe in Gale's arms he straightened himself up and turned to climb through himself when there was an explosion in the hall outside the laundry room door flew off of its hinges, the splintered deadbolt soared like a bullet across the room striking Collings on the shoulder, where it deflected off into the wall embedding itself in the masonry, the pain was unbearable he instinctively looked to see the damage, that was causing his shoulder to throb painfully, his heart was in his throat, numb as he was an eerily agonising feeling swam across his shoulders, a pain that should have overwhelmed him instead it held him fast to the spot.

His right arm was hanging limply by his side attached by the smallest possible amount of sinew, blood dripped from the gaping wound.

'Collings? Are you o-,' Gale's voice called from below, he was looking up and could see the blood dripping from above, he called again more urgency in his voice 'Collings! Come *on!*'

Weakly Collings managed to pull himself back to his senses place his foot on the top rung of the ladder, but he slipped on the blood that had dappled the rung and dropped through the hole, he landed on something soft and wet his arm landing delicately next to him with a splatter. Aurora continued to wail Gale's horrified face came momentarily into focus before it faded in front of him, reappearing then fading again as he tried to keep his eyes open. Finally, the pain from where his arm had detached, consumed him, forcing his eyes closed into an unwelcome sleep, the last thing he could remember was a strange burning where his arm used to be.

Greg

'GRAYSON! HOW MANY TIMES DO I HAVE TO TELL YOU? THAT IS NOT HOW YOU SET A SHOE!' Felix Towe shouted as the horse kicked out, its metal shoe hitting the young boy in the thigh.

The farmer may have been old but for the poor simpleton stableboy, he was still very intimidating.

Grayson cowered away from the farmer fearing another lashing, he'd had too many of them recently, holding his hands up to his face to protect himself but it never came.

'Father leave the poor boy be, it takes him a little while to get his head round such things, he'll get it you just have to give him time'

Grayson lowered his hands to see the beautiful farmer's daughter Margaret, she was scolding her father but even when she was angry Greg thought she was extremely pretty.

Her was a mousy brown and tightly wound in thick curls, that fell gracefully to her shoulders. Today she was wearing a simple blue with large white circular embellishments dotted here and there. Margaret was seven months pregnant and it showed, though she bore it well and any sign of the weight tiring her went unnoticed.

'Just go and check on Ben he was messing about with that tractor again, last I saw of him, it's a wonder the bleeding thing will ever work if he keeps screwing around with it like he does,' her voice was stern and motherly, and it seemed like the old farmer respected that, lowering his head he marched out of the barn muttering curses under his breath.

The young farmhand exhaled in relief drawing her attention, her eyebrows were creased into a frown but when she saw Greg her familiar kind expression returned.

'Oh, Greg why do you let him collar you so? Come on I'll show you again, maybe you just need softer guidance,' her voice was delicate and airy almost singsong this was something Greg had always found so calming.

She walked round the front of the horse and calming it with that same delicate voice and moved to its side gesturing for Greg to join her, she got him to hold the horse's leg up like he had been shown many times before only this time he listened, he didn't want to get it wrong now, this time he was going to remember, he always remembered what the farmer's daughter taught him.

She touched his hand, making his face turn pink he promptly pulled it away, 'aww Greg don't be shy, I won't *hurt* you, you know *that*,' she whispered in his already pink ear, which slowly grew a fiercer shade of red as her breath tickled it.

Together they set the last two horseshoes and they set them right, when they finished he looked at Margaret ready to say something but his mouth just opened and closed like a goldfish with no words finding their way out to hang in the air between them making him appear extremely gormless, more so than usual.

She laughed a beautiful laugh 'Sorry Greg, what was that?' Her eyes were lined with happiness the same happiness she wore every time she saw Greg.

'I-I-I did good? Miss Margaret,' his voice came out thick and dumb a complete contrast to his handsome features he have never fully grasped how to talk properly, being orphaned at a very young age meant he missed out on school and had to learn from hearing other people exchanging their conversations fast and fluent.

She laughed again 'you did brilliantly Greg and less of the miss, I *told* you called me *Mary*,' she smiled again as she kissed him not on the cheek like other women did but on the lips, just like she did that one night under the stars seven months ago, she pulled away and her magnificent Hazel eyes met his pale blue ones.

'Father still doesn't know that it's yours,' she whispered gleefully holding the large bump on her front tugging his hand so he could feel 'I will tell him one day... just not yet, I don't think he will take it well,' there was a firm and noticeable kick from within and Greg flinched, she pulled him out of the barn by his wrist, her grip was light and gentle and it made Greg smile, he loved her and no one would take that away from him.

It was late afternoon and the sun was settling in over the many fields of Felix Towe's farm it looked wonderful as the rays danced across the lake that rippled in the distance.

Greg could see Felix Towe shouting at his son about two hundred yards away as he fiddled with the old tractor, another smile crept across his face at this, he didn't like Benjamin much, he was always teasing Greg about the way that he spoke.

Mary tugged him in the direction of the house and he followed, when they were in the kitchen she turned to him, beaming away.

Greg felt like he was dreaming but it felt too real.

'*We*! are going to start dinner and *I* want you to help,' with that she winked and began rummaging around in the cupboards, pulling out various bowls and pans and setting them here and there on the worktop, 'we're going to be making a roast, with some of the lamb and veg you helped father harvest the other day,' she finished heaving a large slab of meat out of the refrigerator, letting it flop down onto the cold surface.

Before they could start the door burst open and Felix stormed in grabbing Greg by the ear he marched him out of the house silent and rough, across the fields across one into another and then into the corner where up against the old, rusted water trough Greg saw the farmers old shotgun.

Fear gripped him and he began to struggle was the old man going to put him down? The farmer wheeled him about his heavily whiskered face masked the expression of anger hiding beneath.

'YOU WERE IN CHARGE OF THE CATTLE TODAY WERE YOU NOT?' he screamed his words hammering at Greg as he flinched with every syllable as they were spat at his face, the old man's eyebrows furrowed menacingly.

Greg nodded gormlessly 'well I suggest you take a look over there!' the farmer twitched his head towards the hedge line where the field sloped down into a steep ditch, the timid Stableboy edged his way towards it occasionally glancing over his shoulder as the old man close on his heels gun in hand.

Peering over the edge he saw Felix's prize heifer Buttercup keeled over on her side, she was still alive but was bleeding from a very large open wound in her hindquarters, as if something had attacked her and her breathing was harsh, she was in pain as she mooed faintly.

'Now I'm going to have to put her down,' the old man spluttered, it didn't show but Greg somehow knew he was upset.

'I'm s-sorry mister T-Towe,' he stammered he was so scared of the old man he hoped his apology would suffice.

'It's not your fault Greg,' the farmer sighed 'I'm sorry for how I've been lately ever since Aggie died I've not been meself,' he sniffed the air fighting back tears that were starting to shine in the corners of his eyes, 'Buttercup was in a way a solace, summit ter take my mind off of it all yaknow,' he ended.

He shook the tears off hand the gun to Greg before he slipped himself down gracefully moving towards the cow, he called for Greg to hand down his gun, he positioned himself in front of her where he began whispering something to her and ended by kissing the animal on the forehead and stepped back a few feet.

With a loud bang the creature was laid to rest, the old man handed Greg back the gun, Greg took it and watched as the old man quickly turned around his attention focusing on something rustling the other side of the hedge.

Greg saw it better from his higher position, it was another man, but it was moving strangely not like normal humans 'I-I-I don't like it mister, grab my hand,' he Stammered throwing his hand out in front of him his master grabbed it and Greg pulled him up as the other man pushed himself through the thicket tearing off pieces of clothing as it went, scratching away at greyed skin cutting it but blood did not spill from the openings. Greg had never seen anything like it, who was this trespasser? And why was he here?

The man was grabbing up at them gnashing exposed teeth, clawing at them, he was drenched in a red blood the shone in the rays of the setting sun.

'WHO THE HELL ARE YA? AND WHAT THE HELL DO YOU WANT?' Felix's voice was back to its usual sternness as he took the gun from Greg aiming it at the strange man who didn't seem at all scared of the shotgun like Greg was and continued to grasp the air hungrily in front of him.

'I WILL SHOOT, YOU ARE ON MY LAND AND IT IS MY RIGHT TO DO WITH YOU WHAT I WILL!' Felix was shaking with anger Greg thought the old man stepped forward teetering on the edge of the slope the creature began to sound more excited almost like it was being teased like some animal.

'I SWEAR THIS IS YOU LAST WAR-' Felix slipped and quickly started sliding down the slope towards the snarling man below Greg threw himself forward to grasp hold of his master's shoulder just in time, he was heavy and Greg had no idea how long he could hold him there like this, let alone pull him up.

Lucy IIII

The pain in her foot woke her, she was slumped up against the incline that she had just run down, she was alone looking left and right there was nothing except an empty road, the once busy motorway was now completely bare.

Grabbing the gun at her side she pushed herself up using the steep wall like hill as a support, she looked left and right wondering which way was safer away from any biters, she tucked the gun away into the pouch of her hoodie, a thought occurred to her *head to the coast* and she scoured the street for any form of sign that would tell her where to go.

She could smell an electrical burning aroma winding its way to her in the already foul-smelling air, she saw smoke not too far away over another steep graffitied wall opposite, to the left further down the road was a sign, looking the sign over she saw that showed directions to the zoo once again to the left, and straight on was the harbour seafront with the number 5 next to it, *5 miles* she looked at her ruined foot *can I even get that far?*

She put pressure on it but it gave way gingerly beneath her it was clear that she wasn't going to get far let alone 5 miles she tried to hop but the was more difficult the further she moved as the incline came to an end she had nothing to use for support.

Cursing under her breath she inhaled sharply forcing herself to use her damaged foot, she could feel the bones moving around as she place her weight on it, she heaved at the agony but forced herself beyond it and limped on.

She had been limping for about 10 minutes when she could no longer feel the entire leg through a horrid numbness, she welcomed it but then the pins and needles struck making it even more uncomfortable.

She had to stop but where there were some vehicles up ahead there were movements in between them, more biters she thought, studying them carefully.

She withdrew the gun, preparing herself for confrontation there were two of them, one appeared to be standing idly as the other seemed to be feasting on its newly captured prey, he leg began to throb.

There's only two she thought but shed have to get closer to get a good shot, her foot had settled and the pain erupted out of it again but ignoring it she forced herself forwards.

The biters were stood next to each other now but no... were they even biters at all? they were people her heart rose and she pulled her limp leg onwards towards them, moveable as fast as her twisted foot would allow her.

She could make them out clearer now, an old man and a younger one, the older one was walking away now, but the younger one was looking right at her.

He raised something in his hands and aimed it at her, it was a gun! her heart rose more this time in fear she had to tell him she wasn't a biter she had to communicate with him somehow.

She threw her arms up waving she felt silly but if it worked it meant the difference between life or death, thankfully after a moment the man lowered his gun and stepped closer.
'Who are you?!' He called his sandy hair swept to one side bounced as he spoke, the older man turned round behind him, he was running towards her now.

'L-Lucy Braithwaite,' she called back, this was all he needed as he moved towards her quickly, when he was next to her she could see him properly, wow she thought he's really cute, she blushed without realising why was she thinking such a silly thing now of all times? He must have noticed as he spoke.

'Sun must've caught ya, you're all pink,' he joked but she could hear sadness in his voice, he pulled her arm over his shoulder and helped her back towards the older man and their vehicles.

They walked past a body on the floor who was clearly dead he resembled the older man in looks and she assumed that it was his son.
She decided not to question it but instead turned to the man holding her 'so, you know who I am what I'd like to know is who *you* are?,' she asked a peculiar slyness in her voice.

He grinned but responded anyway 'I'm Jack Connors,' she heard an air of mimicry in his voice but she didn't mind his voice sounded as though he sang way back in the other time 'and that is Alan... don't know his last name but he has a wife, her names Elizabeth but prefers Liz or Lizzie and a so-' he cut short, biting his lip guiltily, but Lucy assumed she knew why he was going to say son and it confirmed what she had assumed about the body behind them.

'Is that all?' She prompted further 'only you kinda stopped abruptly,' she sounded like Allison when she used nose her way into conversation, the thought of her sister brought a fleeting tear to her eye, she blinked it away before he noticed.

'Oh what no... there's Aaron *Klennford*? I think and his dog called Shep he's about twelve I think but he hasn't said,' he finished with a subtle nod as if he was checking he hadn't missed anyone off.

When he looked away she wiped the tear from her eye before Jack could noticed as they approached the old man, his face was kind but lined into it was an air of recent obtained grief, again she thought best not to ask.

'What were you doing out here on your own? It's clearly not safe... especially not for someone your age,' his words were gentle and true and she looked at him tears in her eyes she couldn't fight them back anymore.

'M-me and my s-sister were at the zoo, f-for our birthday w-when everything happened and s-she -' she stopped she could tell by the way Jack's arm tightened around her and how Alan nodded solemnly that they understood, she hated how the curtain of composure just dropped and her lip trembled as if she was a large baby.

Jack helped her towards the car opening the door so she could sit down, relieving the pressure from her fractured foot she gently lowered herself into it, he disappeared returning with a bottle of water and some crisps he had rustled up out of the car's boot.

'So, what happened to your foot?' he asked curiously squatting down on the road before her, she noticed his hand was bandaged and the fabric was unmistakably stained with blood.

'I'll tell you if you tell me what happened to your hand,' with the deal struck they exchanged stories, Jack clearly understood the trauma of losing family as he too had to end his own brother *and* his mother, he told her how he'd cut his hand and didn't spare on the detail, apologising about the detail he went into he didn't normal talk so much to anyone, stopping only when he had told her how they had all met.

Lucy held onto every word wondering how he could still smile after all he had gone through in such a small space of time, she admired him he was clearly able to hold himself together.

176

'Now its your turn,' he encouraged 'it really helps to talk it out... trust me,' so she told him about how she had saved her sister only to lose her the moment they reunited and how she had been forced for her own sake to slide down the incline resulting in the now useless foot.

'Try not to put any more pressure on it, for now at least, we have plenty of room in our convoy so... I'm happy to have you tag along and I'm sure the others won't argue against that!' he rose slowly, 'I need to go speak with Al, just sit here for a bit and eat up, when was the last time you ate properly?' she told him it had been an ice cream the previous afternoon so he went back to the boot and pulled various goodies from it for her and lay them on the seat next to her 'you must be starving help yourself, but try not to eat too much, it has to last!' he turned away 'right Alan...' he sighed softly and hung his head for a second before stepping back and turning toward the caravan and vanishing from view.

She ate in silence for a moment, when she heard Jack and Alan's voices moving closer, they were talking in hushed voices but she was able to pick up what Jack was saying as they reappeared from behind the mobile home.

'I understand we need to get moving but you of all people should know that we *can't just* leave him out here in the open we have to bury him or something,' he whispered the old man just responded with a soft nod of his head.

Lucy thought back to her sister's lifeless body at the zoo new tears forming in her eyes she didn't even think to bury her, she just ran, but would she have really been able to do it, given the circumstances, the zoo was packed with the undead out here there were none in sight.

The two men eventually decided that they were going to find a more suitable place and moved the body into the caravan, with the small boy Aaron that Jack had mentioned earlier bringing his dog into the smaller car.

As he hopped into the back of the car Aaron asked 'So, *Jack* is this your *girlfriend?* She's pretty... not like Jacqui though,' Lucy couldn't help but notice it was not only her that blushed, Jack had too.

'Is Jacqui *your* girlfriend? Then Aaron,' Lucy called from the front seat the grin vanished from the boy's face and he was silenced.

Jack chuckled looking at Aaron in the rear-view mirror 'careful what you say bud, you never know what other people might say,' and with that he started the engine and the car moved forward.

They pulled up at the edge of the motorway a few miles later and buried the body of Alan's son beneath a young Oak tree, Alan consoled a distraught Lizzie as Jack carved the name 'Brad,' into the bark shell of the tree, looking over his shoulder to see if he had done a good job.

'Crawley,' Lizzie called through tears that blotched her face answering Jack's look of confusion 'it's our surname,' she added and resumed her position on Alan's shoulder.

Lucy had remained in the car with Shep after all she couldn't move as her foot was in no state to bear any form of weight at all.

The others returned to the vehicles moments later and wee off again, as they rounded a gentle curve a small seaside town loomed over them the streets seemed derelict and empty a few cars scattered here and there but no biters.

The streets twisted and turned through the town they eventually reached the harbour but to their disappointment it was devoid of any salvageable boats or ships all the was left were all wrecks scattered here there and everywhere floating on the murky surface amongst them were pieces of wood and debris.

Jack punched the steering wheel in anger several times sounding the horn in time with his cursing, it all fell silent except the sound of gurgling waves lashing against the shore, which drifted in through the open window, but with it there was something else, a low rumbling noise.

Then something in the mirror caught Lucy's eye something was moving behind them something *big*! It moved slowly towards them, the sun was setting and she couldn't make out any other details.

Jack flicked the headlights on and spun the steering wheel around ready to set off when the lights fell on what she had seen in the reflective surface of the mirror, moments before.

Abigail II

Why was she running *towards* the screams? Abi thought to herself as she pelted past the clearing, where Jake's body was, she didn't dare look upon the ruin that was once her friend, if she had she would have noticed that it was gone, only his jeans lay discarded on the leaf-strewn floor.

She carried on running until she saw the creature bearing down on its prey, Danni had fallen and was on the floor crawling backwards away from her attacker, or *attackers?* There were two of them now, Abi gasped as she recognised the second one, it was Jake his bare legs exposed he was stalking his girlfriend and not in the cute playful way he always had.

There wasn't any time to take the scene in she had to save her Danni somehow. She found a pile of wood to her left and pulled a heavy-set branch from it, she was just strong enough to raise the branch and swung it hard, shouting as she hit her first target, it struck the first creature in the ribs knocking it over where its head collided on a tree bursting open on impact spilling a brownish grey mixture onto the forest floor.

The newly resurrected Jake had heard her yell turning away from Danni and started towards Abi, when he was facing her she could she the wound in his neck where the other one had torn away the flesh and now left the bone exposed, the wound in his stomach was empty as all of his organs had obviously fallen out leaving an empty cavity as its contents dragged across the floor at his feet.

He was so close the metallic smell of blood pushed its way into her nostrils, pulling the branch up again she went to swing it, when Jake's head snapped to one side and he fell forward revealing, a panting and teary-eyed Danni.

She was holding a bloodstained rock using both hands to support it, Jake's body began squirming again and Danni dropped the heavy rock in shock it landed on his head and they watched as blood had started to seep out from under it, the body had stopped moving and like the other one Jake's kill and thankfully remained still.

'What the *hell* just happened?!' Gasped Danni, this was not what Abi was expecting, not in the slightest she had been thinking it was one of their jokes, but it can't have been as two people lay dead in front of them, one of them being an old friend, a friend she had known since secondary school.

She watched as Danni began to realise that Jake was dead tears making their way through the dirt covering her pale features pooling on the underside of her trembling chin.

Abi pulled her friend into a hug and let her cry, 'let it all out,' she whispered through gritted teeth 'Danni... we need to move,' out of the corner of her eye she had noticed movement, turning to look she saw it was another person its clothes were stained with blood and it was heading straight towards them.

It staggered from side to side as if it was drunk, this with the blood made Abi uncertain,

Danni pulled herself away to look, they exchanged a brief look and turned to run this time in the same direction.

They ran fast their bodies surging with a numbing adrenaline as they jumped over exposed roots and dodging low branches.

Abi felt something catch her ankle and felt it pull her backwards and fling her high in the air where she was suspended nearly two metres off of the ground, by a rope bound tightly wrapped around her ankle.

Danni was beneath her 'I'll find some help,' she called and she set off their pursuers staggering blindly behind them.

From her vantage point Abi was able to see that it was male covered in browning blood and bits of organ none of which were his own, as far as she could tell he was unharmed, dressed in military camouflage and there was a gas mask hanging from his neck, she could make out a red insignia on his shoulder that stood out from the brown mess upon his shoulders, but from where she was she couldn't quite make it out fully, before she could do anything he had stumbled off after her friend, leaving her dangling uselessly.

She was completely helpless just hanging there swinging gently, blood rushing into her head, her black hair hanging from it like a bat.

A rustle of leaves in the distance slowly, muffled by the pounding in her ears, her vision began to blur and then beneath her appeared another of those creatures.

Through bleary eyes she could've sworn it was her husband Tom, holding his hands up to catch her, to save her, his breathing was a gurgling snarl and she twitch helpless as cold fingers brushed at her hanging arms she withdrew them, forcing her vision to focus on who was below her.

It wasn't Tom it was somebody she had never seen before and she could scarcely make out any distinguishable feature under a heavy spattering of blood guttering from its mouth, she pushed her hands under her belt securing them in place as she could feel the light headedness as she passed out.

Her unconscious mind skipped from one worry to the next, from Aaron at home, to Tom looking for the dog and on Danni being chased by the soldier, then imagined Danni being attacked in a similar way to Jake and her eyes snapped open gazing down she saw that another two of the creatures had joined the first trying to grab at her even if she fell she was a goner, there was a crunching sound like a bullet cutting through bone beneath her and one of the creatures fell to the floor the other two took no notice, scabbling arms held skywards reaching up to her like adoring fans at a rock concert.

She pulled her arms out of her belt as they were starting to go numb in time to see the other two floor with the same sound as the first.

Somewhere she could hear a young baby crying when suddenly she began to fall she landed on the heap of blood drenched bodies her arms flailing helplessly.

Gale 1

Collings was just lying there, his shoulder in tatters and his right arm was floating in the green sludge next to him, the baby in Gale's arms was bawling her eyes out.

He tried shushing her, it worked but only for a few seconds, so he rocked her back and forth in his arms and gradually she began to yawn and she fell asleep.

Now what was he going to do with collings? He turned to the man lying in the sewage who passed out from the pain in his shoulder, Gale nudged his companion with an outstretched foot, Collings did not respond, he was propped up on a mound of sewage and the wound where his arm once hung was bleeding heavily.

He had to stem it somehow but he was holding a baby, 'now where can I put you,' he whispered to the bundle in his arms, fast asleep she was something so pure and for a moment he had forgotten about the carnage above.

He had an idea, unzipping his camouflage jacket he placed the baby carefully inside zipping it up enough to support her freeing his arms to tend to his fallen comrade.

Kneeling down next to Collings he tore one of his sleeves off and pressed it to the wound, he had no idea what to do next, he had no medical experience at all, the only person in their squadron who *had* any idea what he should do was currently lying unconscious before him with only one arm.

All he knew was to apply pressure, pushing Collings onto his side he grabbed at the pack beneath him, he was only after something like a bandage something to hold over the wound at least until they could find an alternative.

He found one right at the bottom of the small bag and set about wrapping Collings up, when he finished he was pleased at the attempt he had made, at least you can't see the wound anymore he thought.

Pulling his water cannister out he raised it to his mouth but was struck by yet another idea, he splashed the water over Collings' face, waking him up with a weak spluttering, his eyes were wide and it looked as though he wanted to scream but he just sat up and looked and the dressing Gale had just applied, laughing weakly.

'Aww damn... I was kinda fond of that one,' he joked deliriously 'need to get the wound sealed before I bleed out or get an infection... You got anything that can start a fire?'

Gale, shocked at his colleague's strange behaviour searched his pockets pulling out Hendry's old zippo lighter, he turned it in his hand, thinking about what happened in the bathroom previously 'he was going to be my brother-in-law you know,' he sighed 'he gave me this before we came here,' he ran his index finger down the intricate design of a Chinese dragon engraved into the metal on one side.

'I'm sorry Gale I didn't... it wasn't my intention,' Collings replied he knew about that lighter Hendry and he had joined up together he had known him since they were little, they had always done so much together including enlisting in the military and Gale was set to marry Hendry's sister before they received the orders to deal with the dead.

'I know... it's just difficult, everyone's dying around us it's a lot to deal with all of a sudden,' he wasn't finished 'I know we're soldiers and we're trained to be tough but... I'm actually pretty scared,' his words hung in the air and Collings looked thoughtfully at his companion for a second 'I'm scared we're not going to make it out of this and I'm scared that I'll never see Alice again.

'I'm scared too Gale, actually I'm fucking *terrified* not just for us but for that little girl and anyone else that's still out there, I'm also concerned that my arm is floating in shit and not where it should be...' he sounded extremely dismayed by this but he continued, 'do we have anything flat? Metal and most importantly clean?' This request was more confusing than the first and it came suddenly but Gale didn't think to question it.

Looking at Collings he noticed that he was wearing a large flat belt buckle pointing at it Collings looked down to see what he was pointing at 'what about yours?'

'Kinda using it the hold Aurora in place, keeping my hands free and the baby safe,' Gale responded. Collings let out a whoop of weak laughter removed his belt buckle with a degree of difficulty with his sole had and held it out to Gale.

'Right... We need to get the hell outta here,' Collings spoke as he hauled himself up swaying slightly he was ablet to balance himself, considering he had just lost his arm he still had a lot of energy in him.

'Why though I thought we were sealing the wound,' Gale asked as he stumbled across to help steady him.

'We are but this sewer is full of shit and where there's shit there's methane gas and we need fire, do you get where I'm heading?' Gale put two and two together he should have known that. He pocketed the belt buckle and the lighter.

'Want me to grab righty?' He asked pointing to the arm floating in the muck, which had begun sinking slowly.

Collings just shook his head and turned away his face pale in the faint light, he walked down the pipe-way with Gale jogging behind clumsily him.

They had been slipping about in the sewer for a while before then managed to find any form of way out and even then all they managed to find was a street full of creepers.

Gale stepped down from the last rung of the ladder shaking his head for the third time, the tunnel turned to the left sharply ahead and they had no choice but to follow it.

Up ahead was an opening they moved towards it they had made it the main sewer outlet which meant clean air, Gale went ahead peering out into a forest the pipe opening out above a river along its edge.

Collings drew level with him his face was as white as a sheet he sat on the lip of the pipe 'right... now we can cauterise Mr. stumpy,' a faint smile appeared on his face as he looked up to Gale, beneath the transparent smile Gale saw the ghost of a conflicting expression but ignored it.

Gale looked at him with the same blank expression, he knew what cauterising was but how no idea how he would even go about it.

'First u need to start a fire,' Collings breathed answering the unasked question, 'a small one will be fine, we're by a wood so kindling should be easy enough to find.'

Gale unzipped his jacket pulling the small child from within carefully passing it the Collings who adjusted himself so he could cradle her in his lap. Gale disappeared into the wood reappearing seconds later with arms full of twigs and dried leaves, he made a small pile and pulled the lighter from his pocket, he tried to light the pile but it would simply smoke shortly before extinguishing 'you should use one of those rags!' Collings called from his ledge, Gale did as he suggested holding the cloth over the flame it caught quicker than he expected and the flames danced in his eyes, he lowered the cloth into the makeshift fire he had assembled and the debris he collected slowly caught ablaze.

'Now heat the buckle in the embers, it'll be red hot so you may need to use something to hold it with,' Collings whispered and he pulled his pack from behind him with his remaining hand, 'there should be some pliers in there you need to close the arteries first though, heat the end of them and seal it with them,' he finished.

Gale did as he was told the fire was hotter than he assumed it would be, he wiped the pooling sweat from his face, Collings had already removing the bodged sling revealing the open wound Gale used the pliers to pinch the arteries closing them, Collings yelled in agony but urged him to carry on regardless, his shout woke the sleeping child who began to wail, even though he was clearly in agony Colling kept a firm grip on her trying to calm her through each anguished breath.

'Now use the alcohol in the pack and another rag to sterilise the wound,' Gale did as instructed Collings screamed through a closed mouth, eyes watering.

Gale returned to the fire using the pliers to pick the buckle up which had been sitting in the fire for long enough that it was glowing red now and promptly pressed it to the stump of collings' arm using his remaining sleeve which he bundled up and soaked in water, he could hear the skin hissing beneath the metal and the smell of his friends burning skin reminded him of cooked pork, enticed his nostrils he removed the buckle and the raw burned flesh had melted together to hide the exposed artery beneath; it looked far more serious than it was, 'Fuck! I forgot how much that hurts,' Collings cursed making Gale wonder when else had he had to do such a thing, 'have you got any water?' Collings finished allowing Gale to take Aurora from him.

Gale surrendered his canteen and Collings drained it, he stood up and made his way down to the forest floor, even with only one arm he made it look easy, Gale was surprised he had not passed out.

Gale followed supporting the small child once again tucked away inside his jacket. He descended the rocks far less gracefully joining Collings at their base, when they reached the floor they set off.

It wasn't long before they came across more creepers three of them reaching up for something hanging from a tree, they couldn't see what as it was beyond their vision, at that point Aurora began to cry, drawing the attention of the creepers toward them.

 Alice I

The sun hung high in the sky, beating down on the Tarmac below, waves of heat releasing themselves from the dense black surface sending them zigzagging into the air above.

The low rumble of a motorcycle sounded in the distance drawing the attention of several staggering shapes dotted across the barren road, wandering aimlessly towards the noise.

As the bike passed, the shapes swarmed towards it, like moths to a flame, the rider swatting them aside with a heavily metal pipe forcing them to tumble onto the scorching pavement melting to it in the intense heat.

The bike charged forward leaving the shapes lying there, pulling over to one side its rider placed the pipe into a leg restraint and removed their black helmet, revealing a long stream of dark hair and the face of a woman several piercings lined her left eyebrow and a single labret clung to the right side of her bright purple bottom lip.

Setting the bike stand down with a kick the rumbling engine silenced itself. She removed a walkie talkie from her belt, pressing the call button on the side, she raised it to her mouth and spoke.

'Harritosis this is Axel-rod the coast is clear... over,' A crackle of static hissed out of the speaker, she released the button it beeped to signal the end of the message.

'We never agreed those codenames Alice, just call me by my *proper* name, either way I'll be there in a jiffy... over,' a man's voice burst out of the speaker in response, followed by more static and the compulsory sign off beep.

Alice clipped the device back onto her belt, waiting, the day was hot and she was wearing her full leathers, it was unbearable, raising her hand she unzipped her heavy jacket, removing it with difficulty, sweat forcing it to cling to her skin, finally she relieved herself from it, the tight tank top crumpling slightly to reveal a small heart tattoo on hir hip as she cast the jacket onto the floor along with her helmet.

Swinging herself off of the large frame of her bike she stretched her arms above her head stretching herself feeling the satisfactory pop of her spine she rocked her head side to side. She removed a lollipop from her back pocket, unwrapping it she threw the wrapper to one side, popping it into her mouth *my blue-raspberry* she leaned on her bike, waiting for her companion.

'*Come on*! Hari,' she gasped after about thirty minutes had come and gone, her golden speckled green eyes surveying the horizon for any movement, he always took his time, well truthfully she'd only really known him for just under a week, ever since the world went to shit... but that was enough time to realise that he liked to be precise about everything and took his time in doing so.

The sound of an engine reached her ears and she looked back down the street to the hill where she had come from, in time to see a large white van heading towards her, he'd done it she thought, pushing herself of the bike and jumping up and down in the middle of the road arms waving above her head.

As the van crested the brow of the hill she saw to her horror the horde of shapes pursuing it hundreds of the dead chasing the van like kids chasing an ice cream truck, in the good old days, but this was no summer holiday, this was far more sinister.

Eyes widening in horror, she had no time to grab her gear instead she flung herself onto the bike kicked up the stand and kicked out to start it up, it spluttered into life and she accelerated away from the van and the mass of hungry followers.

'Picked up a bit of a following... sorry... over,' Harrito's voice sounded muffled over the noise of the motorcycle, Alice ignored it speeding on up another hill.

Pulling the pipe from its restraint she downed more creatures loitering around the street the speed of the bike adding to the force of her strikes smashing their skulls as she passed.
The van trundled on behind her grinding the bodies into the Tarmac, she swung the pipe once

again she missing as it lunged toward her dodging the blow turning her head she watched and the van slammed into it, blood splattered over the windscreen, fragments of the body lodging themselves into the wipers, rendering them useless leaving the driver blind she watched as it swerved sideways toppling into a ditch to the side of the road.

Looking beyond the wreck she noticed they had put enough distance between themselves and the crowd that she could turn back and help Harrito, make a sharp u-turn she aimed the bike towards the protruding edge of the overturned van, speeding towards it.

'HARRI ARE YOU OK?!' She called as she prop the bike up she dropped herself into the ditch next to the van looking through the smashed windscreen.

The small form of Harrito was sat wide eyed still clinging onto the steering wheel 'I think... you missed one,' he muttered releasing the wheel and unclicking his seatbelt.

Harrito was a small Asian man, he was very agile and he clambered out through the windscreen with ease landing next the Alice, who was a great deal taller than him. 'I gotta go back on your bike now haven't I?' He grumbled looking up at her through a pair of dark brown eyes that were magnified by a pair of thick glasses, she laughed with a nod as they climbed up the slope.

They both mounted the bike and Alice kicked at the kick start, but the bike spluttered and died, she looked down the road behind the van the wall of the dead was about one hundred yards away, she kicked again and once again it spluttered into nothing, they were less the 80 yards away now.

'COME ON! COME ON!' she urged kicking out once again, still nothing they were very close now and others were closing in from all angles, Harrito was clinging hard onto her back.

'Your useless machine is going to get us killed!' he wailed as the dead moved in.

Andrew

Andrew read the final pane of the comic book for a third time, dropping it to the floor in frustration, he already knew that it finished on a cliff-hanger, yet it was the only thing he could do to pass the time.

He pushed a mass of long blonde hair back from off his face, revealing one brown and one green eye, before allowing it to drop and cover the latter of the two, he bit his lip ring in annoyance, lowering his head to look down at the floor.

His school bag lay open at his feet sweet wrappers and empty bottles of water strewn across the elevator around it, he'd been trapped in here for several days now and he had given up hope of rescue, he was going insane there was no one about all he could remember was people attacking each other.

All thoughts of rescue had gone out of the window when the elevator stopped the doors stood ajar the smallest gap between them, enough to reveal the inside of the shaft and about a foot of the floor below, it had dropped steadily by half a floor already and Andrew did not feel ready for it to fall anymore.

He tried calling for help but the people on that floor just snarled and clawed at the small opening this scared him, he had even gone as far as to pee through the gap as he no place else to go, he was glad that it was only the water taking effect but he was sure that it wouldn't be long before the other side of nature called, he had eaten a lot of snickers bars after all, he pushed the thought as far back as he could, not enjoying the thought of them making a sudden reappearance, not now.

He dropped himself carefully onto the floor with a sigh, he wanted to get out but with every second he could feel a growing fear that he was going to die here, trapped like an animal in a zoo, he pulled a pen and some paper out of his bag and wrote 'My name is Andrew (Andy) Dagg, I am stuck, please help!'

He posted the page through the hole watching it fall onto the floor below, a fruitless attempt of an S.O.S but maybe somebody was still out there.

'Fifteen years old and you're going to die trapped inside a *lift*, during a zombie apocalypse' he whispered to himself as another gurgling Zombie shuffled past the door, he knew what they were he'd played enough video games to know a zombie when he saw one, he just never though it could actually happen not like this.

He had been attending a work experience course at the big video game company across the road from his school and he was loving it, well... that was until the lift broke down, now he was living in a real-life video game.

He was too tired to think, he could feel his eyes begin to droop, as he began to fall ever so gradually asleep, when he remembered the can of energy drink sitting at the bottom of his bag, he had avoided drinking it up till now, knowing all too well, even opening it would draw the attention of the dead outside, but at least it would keep himself up for a little while longer, but staying awake was the best option available, as he felt the lift shift another centi-metre.

He opened the can with an audible hiss, as he had imagined the sound drew the attention of the gurgling man who was now once again trying to claw its way into the small room. Andy downed the can and burped loudly throwing the empty vessel out through the opening the creature below moving towards the clang as it hit the wall opposite.

He tilted his head backwards resting it on the wooden veneer wall of the lift, the sooner his crown met the vertical surface the sooner he saw it, the emergency hatch! Set into the metal ceiling.

There was a chance he could climb through it and maybe get off on a safer floor or even onto the roof, he pushed himself to his feet, using the handrail he pulled himself up he was just tall enough to try and push it open, using one arm he unlatched it and pushed at the metal door.

It moved about two inches but was heavier than it looked and required a lot more force than that of his one hand, dropping slowly to the floor he rummaged through his bag searching for something that could help, he found nothing... Turning his attention to the small room around him searching helplessly for anything that would help in anyway.

Beside the doors was the control panel and below the buttons he saw a fire extinguisher! grasping hold of it quickly he resumed his position this time on the corner directly below the hatch using the extinguisher he pushed the small door as high as he could, there was a brief moment where it teetered vertically on its edge before it fell backwards with almighty 'BANG!' causing the whole room to shake.

The Zombie was back at the door but Andy had already pulled himself out onto the roof of the small box, looking up all he could see was a thick dark cloud of smoke, he could make out the rungs of a ladder built into the wall towards the back of the elevator and moved towards them.

He pulled his weight onto them when his foot left the roof, he heard something heavy land onto it with a sickening splat, refusing to look over his shoulder he stared upwards he could feel something wet hit his face but was unable to see what it was or even where it came from in fact he couldn't really see *anything*.

Then another loud thump more liquid splattering him, this time he felt it up his back, still he could see nothing but when he breathed in the smell of rotten meat hung in the air, he counted as a third and a forth object hit the elevator covering him in more of the strange wet stuff he decided he was going to move when a fifth bang hit the roof and the elevator moved as it brake uncoupled at last sending it plummeting down the shaft like a passing train he clung to the ladder as the wind howled past him, when it was safe to do so he pulled himself up, the rungs were wet with the same stuff now covering him.

But he held onto them tightly his feet slipped from side to side but he forced himself upwards, soon he was level with the smoke and was now completely blind, closing his eyes to avoid them stinging he pulled himself further upwards when the ladder stopped he was still enveloped in the thick black fog he couldn't just hang here, he couldn't even *breathe,* his free hand scrambled for something *anything,* after all the effort he couldn't just die *here.*

He flung his arm up searching for anything to pull himself further up, scurrying blindly he found that in front of him was what felt like an alcove, hand still stroking the back wall he found another latch like handle.

He pulled at it and it gave easier than he expected and a door swung open he pulled himself out of it coughing and spluttering as smoke billowed out into the sky above him, he spilled out onto a floor made of small stones that felt warm beneath his hands, he forced his eyes open to a bright blue blur, blinking repeatedly it took a while for his eyes to adjust, when they did he saw that he had made it onto the roof.

His ears picked up on the sounds of birds singing all around drowning out any of the noise far below, there was another sound far closer than that of the birds the sound of gravel under foot, he sat up looking frantically for cover the noise was coming from behind him moving closer, he was free but he was not alone.

Benjamin

'BAYER WHAT ARE YOU PLA-,' Ben's voice exploded over him 'WHAT IN THE HELL IS THAT THING?!' his voice turned drastically into shock as he dropped to help Greg pull his father away from the snarling creature struggling at the bottom of the ditch.

The three of them looked at the creature bewilderment fresh in the expressions, as the man continued to claw hungrily up at them, they saw that only one of the finished with something that faintly resembled a hand, distorted and missing pieces of fingers, the other arm ended in a crusted bleeding stump, taking in further details they noticed wounds that resembled teeth marks gouged into the man's flesh where his missing hand should have been, similar abrasions cascaded across the pale speckled skin, that lay exposed beneath what remained of his tattered clothing. These marks were far from shallow and as it moved persistently, they could see places where the whitened protuberances of bone sprouted from some of the deeper lesions. Eyes glazed over by a filmy substance giving them a greyish hue, it reached blindly up at them they reflected the sun's light dimly, giving the false element of life to the otherwise lifeless face.

Greg was shaking uncontrollably the fear clearly visible in his face, 'Greg... get indoors tell Mary to stay with you... keep her safe,' Felix's voice was shaking but he appeared calm.

Greg nodded but remained rooted to the spot his eyes fixed on something the other side of the hedge his mouth hanging open, 'BAYER DID YOU NOT HEAR FATHER!' Ben yelled at him but Greg just pointed, his finger trembling aimed somewhere beyond the field's boundary.

Ben traced the line between the two towards the field that was usually full of cows, his mouth fell open and his hazel eyes so like his sister's widened, the field was full of more of these creatures and they seemed to be crouching in circles around the animals within. Ben squinted seeing them tear into the flesh of the livestock they worked so tirelessly to maintain ripping them to pieces with their hands, large pieces brought raw to their mouths chewing greedily.

'Father... there's more of them... afuckofalot more,' he gulped loudly eyes wide fear striking him almost dumb, 'Greg... go protect Mary lock the doors,' he whispered 'father we need to move too, there's no chance in hell we are safe here.'

Greg turned on his heels and ran quickly through the first field and into the next before disappearing into the house, Ben grabbed his father by the shoulder pulling him away, the wounded man snapping at them angrily.

They ran along the same route Greg had used, but the old man started falling behind, into the first field towards the house out of the corner of his eye Ben saw several more things struggling at the barbed fence nearby, arms outstretched in their direction hanging there stupidly he saw as the gate lay wide open.

He turned abruptly forcing his father to stop 'BEN! WHAT THE *HELL* ARE YOU DOING! DO NOT GO ANYWHERE NEAR THOSE THINGS!'

But Felix's voice went unnoticed by his son as he watched him run towards the gate, he turned to the house and back towards his son, and the creatures hanging from the fence.

'DAD... JUST GO! DON'T WORRY ABOUT ME I'LL BE FINE!' Ben yelled as he ran more creatures were making their way up the field towards the open gate he reached it before them, only just, he forced it closed, bolting it to the fence, he felt something sharp clamp down on his arm, horrified he pulled it away from the mouth of the creature that bit him, just in time he saw the bite mark bruised his skin but had not punctured it.

He turned and ran back to the house before anything else could happen, heart pounding somewhere in his throat, his arm throbbing by his side, he heard the strange thing's voices calling behind him, rasping, Snarling, even snapping their teeth as they called, disregarding them he continued to force himself further away from them, in the direction of the door.

His hand was on the door handle before he knew it, it was locked he heard the wood breaking behind him as the gate gave way, under the weight of the creatures as more joined there increasing numbers.

He pounded on the door but they wouldn't be able to lock the door fast enough 'Wait! don't open it,' he called back through the wood as he heard the keys begin to twist in the lock, running round the house to the back that door was locked too, he had to get in somehow, he had to or he could find somewhere else to hide.

The choir of groaning voices was much closer now, he was certain it was coming from the other side of the house they must be very close to it now, looking around he found nothing useful, with no way to get in, the wooden porch was suddenly alight with the sound of footsteps, slow heavy footsteps lots of them, thundering mere metres away.

He could see the barn and it was not too far away and the field between them was clear, making up his mind he ran towards it noticing even from as far as he was that it too was locked, he remembered the keys were jangling away in his dungaree pocket, he was a couple of feet away when he pulled them out, fumbling to find the right one as he ran.

Pulling at the padlock he thrust the key into it twisting the metal anti clockwise, it snapped in his haste, he cursed loudly threw the broken key aside, looking around for another way of removing the now inoperable lock.

An axe was leaning against a tree trunk about two metres away, beyond it he could see more creatures making their way toward him, once again they were caught up in a fence unable to move further, they can't be too smart but they're still dangerous. Why was this happening? he rushed towards the axe snatching it up and turning back to the large red building, breathing heavily he ran back fatigue pressing in on him, his vision blurring as sweat poured over his face.

The grass had grown unusually long in places and he felt his hand slip on something obscured by it, choosing to overlook it he hastily grabbed hold of the handle of the axe, heaving it onto his shoulder, he hurried back slipping once again on whatever was hidden away deep in the grass, he felt something clasp around his ankle and he rolled onto his back to see what it was, it was one of those things, this one only has a head and arms one of which had a firm hold on his ankle, picking up the heavy axe he hacked at the creature rapidly, hitting the ground carelessly first, if he was careful he would surely lop his own leg from his body, his second swipe was more carefully placed as it hit the skull it fell upon him and Ben scrambled from it returning to his feet, stumbling as too much blood plummeted from his head, dizzying him momentarily.

He reached the locked doors with difficulty, raising the axe, struck the padlock once and then a second time on the third strike it fell to the floor taking the heavy with it releasing the large wooden panels.

218

He pushed his way inside unable to lock the door behind him he looked anxiously around the dark interior, there was a ladder leading to the hayloft at the far end of the structure he moved towards it, reaching out he began pulling himself up with difficulty, still clutching the blood-soaked axe in his hands, eventually he reached the suspended me Sonae level at its top breathing heavily.

Perched at the edge of the platform wiping the sweat from his brow when a noise caught his attention from behind him, *What now!* He thought, but before he could turn around something metal hit the back of his head with enough force to knock him out cold.

A man stood over him before dropping to his knees where he checked for wounds, he eyes paused for a moment on the bruised forearm ensuring there was no break in the skin, he saw no trace of blood except for the pool beneath the skin that had purpled the surface, breathing a sigh of relief he returned to his feet, moving swiftly he turned on the spot, strode across the hay sprinkled landing, he lowered himself onto a haybale by the large hayloft door and waited.

Danielle

Danni's footsteps were echoed by her pursuer, she glanced over her shoulder at the man that had become her shadow, only he wasn't there, he'd vanished, slowing to a stop. The heat of newly formed blisters spread all over her feet, she removed her shoe to relieve them, her toes had torn their way through her socks they were ruined!

Something behind made her wheel about a swish of material rubbing together, the man was back and he was closing in on her quickly, arms outstretched, she backed away from him tripping over the discarded shoe on the forest floor, she fell to the ground throwing her arms behind her in an attempt to cushion her fall, now on the floor and vulnerable she began scrambling backwards like a crab when her shoulders hit a tree, she was trapped the man was upon her. But he wasn't biting at her? not like those creatures, not like the thing that had taken Jake from her.

His face though stained with blood was unmarked, his eyes alive, yet she could see behind them, a hunger for more than her meat. He pulled her arms rough and uncaring towards him, then proceeded to bind them loosely allowing him to undress her. all the while he stayed silent as he raped her, she winced as her forced his way inside her, not waiting for her to welcome him. His foul-smelling hand clasped over her mouth stifling any scream, Danni wept as he relentlessly thrust himself inside.

Disgusted and used she tried to bite him but he was ready for her, moving his hand in a way that prevented her teeth gaining purchase, forcing her mouth to stay closed, almost as if he'd *done* this before... he continued to violate her and she felt every little detail of it, numbness would not block it no matter how much she willed it to, she even knew when he had finished; she could feel that too.

Suddenly She saw a shadow on the ground beside them, making its way up the tree beside her head, the shadow swayed as its owner lunged towards them, biting into her attacker's shoulder, she heard his voice for the first time, a strangled agonised yell. He twisted himself around his penis still inside her and she felt more of his fluid spill onto her navel. He threw the creature away from him with ease; his trousers were still down as he pulled himself from her lurching drunkenly to the thing on the floor dropping on top of it, he began punching the skull to a pulp with his bare hands.

Now was her chance she struggled against her bindings, freeing one arm she was able to push herself to her feet, she grabbed at her underwear pulling them up, sullied, scared and *dirty,* she ran leaving her attacker still punching fiercely at the already smashed skull, his hands were hitting the ground now, yelling hysterically.

Ahead of her another two ungainly shapes flitted through the trees making their way towards the shouting behind her, she spun on the spot, scared of what had just happened and what could still happen, she noticed a hollow in a tree nearby. She pelted towards it climbing up to the opening she soon found herself squeezing her slender body through the small split of in the wood and watched from afar as the two shapes, descended on the grief-stricken man still hammering hist fists into the floor.

She watched with a strange combination of horror and satisfaction as blood poured from wounds torn into his skin, still watching as he fell forward onto the forest floor and she watched as the predators tore him apart in frenzied bloodlust, she wept softly as she stared at the scene ahead of her, unable to take her eyes away, she felt sick, but fought back the overpowering need to vomit that was now consuming her.

Memories flooded through her mind of Jake of Abi... *Abi...* in the struggle she had forgotten about her friend strung up in the air by her leg, she had to help her, she had already drawn one away she certainly couldn't draw another two back, but she had to do *something*.

Her focus landed back on the two creatures, still feasting on the remains of the man who was attacking her moments ago, almost celebrating greedily as blood rained from their jaws, there was no way she could pull herself out of here without catching their attention.

A flutter of wings as a bird flew away from the top of the hollowed trunk above, sending dust cascading down upon her, she sneezed uncontrollably, her stomach churned once more as the dead turned their ugly faces in her direction, leaving the ruined body behind they moved in her direction, eagerly anticipating a fresh kill.

Soon their arms were clawing through the crack in the tree, they seemed oblivious to the fact that their skin had started to fall away where the wood cut into them as they fought to be the first to taste her flesh, it dropped out of sight hitting the ground splattering Danni's exposed toes, she was trapped and she had no idea how long the splintering trunk would hold them back.

They persisted the wood cut through their cuts giving the permanent and grotesque grins mutilating them further, the more they moved the more the nausea set into her, she was unable to hold onto it and she gave into its vile embrace.

The bile splattered to the floor over her already blood-soaked feet.

Hysterically she wiped at her face with her sleeve and whimpered, a whimper that burst for in a terrible scream she had given up containing, tears disturbed her already ruined make-up, dripped onto her clothes, she pushed her body as far as she could from the mangled limbs that were mere inches away from her.

She dropped beneath their reach her eye remaining on them making sure she didn't give them the opportunity to catch hold of her.

The smell of her own vomit mixed with the fetor of decay made its way to her nostrils and she hastily pulled the collar of her jumper to mask the putrid scent.

Rupert

Lydia Wescott was sat on a box in the corner, facing the locked door surveying it with her vibrant green eyes, her long blonde hair tied back loosely, several intricate plaits interwoven together meeting to form a unique ponytail that fell neatly beyond her neckline.

To one side of her Rupert Gray paced backwards and forwards to one side, muttering under his breath his dark skin beaded with sweat in the heat.

Everything was silent for the first time in two days, the warmth was pressing in on them making them feel dehydrated, they had exhausted their food supply and any remaining water lay beyond *that* door.

Rupert strode towards it and dropped to one knee, removed its key and peered through the keyhole into the room beyond, the sun was filtering delicately through the blinds hanging over the windows opposite, he could see no sign of movement within the limited line of vision, the room appeared empty.

'I... *think...* the coast is clear,' he straightened up. Returning the key to the lock he unlocked the door with a loud 'click,' and pulled it open only slightly to get a better look, the door was open only a slither when he saw something move on the far side of the room, hurriedly he slammed the door and attempted to lock it in his haste he fumbled the small piece of metal dropped onto the floor, where it hit his foot and slid under the door into the room outside.

Moving away from the door he snatched at the first thing his hands came across his body was too numb to even feel what it was, his eyes remained glued to the door, all of a sudden there was a loud bang as if something big was trying to force its way in, causing the whole wall to shake ominously.

Lydia rose next to him, she was young, not much older than nineteen but she was extremely intelligent; 'It doesn't *seem* clear,' airy and light, but the taunting emphasis was obvious, another bang on the door separating them from the outside world, followed by another, something was trying extremely hard to get to them and it wouldn't give up until it did.

'Excuse me... Rupert? but why are you holding a Superflex ruler?' the same airy sweet voice; Rupert looked down at his hands tearing his gaze away from the door, he noticed that his palms were sweating he was in fact brandishing a fluorescent pink, flexible ruler like a sword, another bang made him jump and his attention returned to the door.

'Our only way out is that way, there appears to only be one of them,' he whispered casting the ruler aside, not taking his eyes off of the door in front of them, as it bang with more force than before, he flinched again his heart rising, its tempo beat an uncomfortable tattoo in his throat.

The door began to creak as the banging grew more aggressive, noting the latch beginning to splinter, as the wood bowed inwards, he dared not blink in case it gave way, he was scared stiff of what was out there it wasn't human, not anymore.

There was a loud crunch as the door burst open as the shape of a small boy fell through it, scrambling to his feet he lunged at them growling and snapping as it approached it knocked Rupert over in a strength not accurate of its form, his teeth clicking together as it tried to bite at him, Rupert's glasses fell onto the floor amidst the commotion, lost in the flurry of paper that cascaded from the shelf above them as they struggled.

Trying his hardest to fend the child off, Rupert held the small body off with his right arm, taking care to avoid those sharp teeth, left hand searching the floor for something to try and knock the thing off, the search it seemed to go on forever, forcing the face away from him all the while, when all of a sudden the small form groaned as its body relaxed and then unmoving.

Pushing the now frail body off of him it fell to the floor onto its back pushing the bundle of pencils through its open mouth, Lydia was stood over him, her hand outstretched signalling for him to take it, which he did, he was on his feet thanking her as he dusted himself off, the first thing he checked was the open door, revealing the room outside.

Rupert was a primary school teacher and as he stepped out of the cupboard he had been stuck in for two days he looked upon the horror of the days before.

Motionless bodies of his young students lay scattered across the floor with tables overturned crushing several of them blood was everywhere, far too much than he would've liked.

He vomited ceremoniously into the nearby waste-paper basket, his body shaking death was not something that had come by frequently, not, at least, in such a gruesome manner as this.

He watched as Lydia moved about closing the wide staring eyes on the terrified faces of the children, - their expressions frozen in their last moments - around the room whispering as she did so, her eyes showed no sign of emotion but he could tell she was upset, it had been the last day of her volunteer placement after all and she had grown attached to many of the children, who now... sadly lay deceased on the classroom floor.

She turned to him after closing the last of the children's eyes not appearing at rest and sleeping peacefully, she sighed wiping a single tear from her eye, as she disappeared back into the cupboard, within seconds she was in the doorway, holding his glasses and a piece of paper, returning his glasses to his face he realised she held the class register.

'Not all of the children are here, three of them are missing,' her voice was soft but he could hear a trace of hope lined into it as she spoke, 'we have to look for them,' she ended hurrying to the door, he hadn't the heart to say what he thought out loud and followed her to the classroom door.

'But Lydia, its most likely not safe out there,' he replied catching up with her and pulling her hand away from the door handle, she looked at him with a look of disgust etched into her fair features.

'But surely Mr Gray you do not expect me to stand idly by as three young children's lives are at risk,' the delicate normality of her tone had gone her voice was raised and fearing, in a weird way Rupert feared this more than anything else, scared she may draw some unwanted attention he attempted hush her.

'Okay, okay we'll look for them but as soon as we can we need to get out of here,' his compromise relaxed her expression and relief flooded through him, he turned his attention to the small window set into the wooden door, looking out onto the corridor beyond.

Lined against the wall opposite were several lockers smeared handprints had decorated them, but there were no signs of anyone out there just a couple of still bodies lying still on the ground tranquil as though in ritual of sleep.

One of them he noticed was one of the three they were looking for, crushed beneath one of the heavy lockers, his skin pale and cold, he turned back to Lydia, she was waiting impatiently behind him.

'Joey Brown is outside the room,' he sighed 'he hasn't made it... that leaves only two,' his voice shook as he fought back the urge to vomit again, he grasped the door handle and opened the door slowly, the corridor was silent as the edged there was into it.

It was only when they passed the lockers that they heard any sound at all, there was a sniff that wormed its way out of one of the metal boxes lining the corridor, it drew their attention and they moved closer to the source of the sound, when a voice screamed out of them.

'NO! NO! PWEASE! NO!' A young girl's voice erupted out of the lower right locker, they moved towards it in haste, the thought of her screams drawing any attention was far from what they needed.

'Shhh calm down we're here to help you,' Lydia whispered through the metal slats at the top of the door, the girl fell silent with the occasional sniff 'can you open the door from that side?' Lydia continued.

'No, I'm stuck miss,' her voice sounded thick through floods of tears.

'Don't worry we'll get you out,' Lydia responded 'Do we have anything to pry the door open?' Her attention turning back to Rupert who shrugged uselessly, a blank look on his face.

'Miss if you can find my fwiend Johnny he had the key, he should still have it,' the idea never occurred to her but sadly she knew exactly where johnny was and turned towards the body of the small boy pinned beneath the overturned locker.

His small hand was balled into a fist around something, and she stooped down to retrieve it, the boys eyes were open staring up at the ceiling his small body crumpled in a heap but there was no clear sign of any damage except a large bruise to his head dried blood leaking from his ears.

It was clear that he died as a result of heavy impact on his head, Rupert watched as she stooped down next to him she closed his eyes he looked at peace, she whispered something again, as she open the small hand revealing a small key, she took it and turned back to the locker with the girl encased inside.

The key worked and the small girl pulled her way out hugging her saviours, she was clutching a small bag in her hands hanging out of it was a floppy eared bunny toy and an empty water bottle.

'Rosie we're so glad you're safe!' Rupert's voice was warm and reassuring, and the small girl looked at him smiling, 'but do you know where Samantha is?' Samantha was the only child unaccounted for and Rosie's best friend.

The girl shook her head and asked, 'did you find Johnny?' Her question was not expected, despite it being the obvious route of conversation, she was very young how could they explain that her friend Johnny was unfortunately lying behind them dead?

But she had already seen him and begun to cry, Lydia picked her up and comforted her as she whimpered into her shoulder, 'we have to move Lydia,' Rupert's voice was urgent only this time she agreed and they headed to the exit, more bodies scattered here and there down the corridor.

They reached the exit and stared out into the playground, it was filled with more like the little boy in the cupboard all different shapes and sizes and there just the other side of the glass was Samantha shuffling amongst the crowd slowly in their direction, soon she was at the window clawing at them weakly.

More tears formed in Rosie's eyes and Lydia hugged her as they stared out at the mass of bodies outside, they were trapped again this time there was no way out.

Jack IV

Jack kept his grip firmly on the wheel staring at what lay ahead of them, he had no idea what to do! He could feel the sweat beneath his hands as the he adjusted his grip on the faux leather steering wheel.

The street in front of them was blocked a large black van, as they watched people began to disembark from it armed with machine guns, they assembled themselves like mercenaries in front of the van aiming their weapons at the car and the caravan behind.

'What do reckon they want?' He muttered more to himself than the others, as a heavily armoured figure appeared, stopping in line with them highlighted by the headlights, they watched as they raised their arm and spoke through a megaphone that was strapped to their wrist.

'Step out of the vehicles with your arms where we can see them,' a woman's voice surly and masculine contaminated with the gravely edge of a heavy smoker reached them, Jack slid his gun instinctively into his pocket noticing out of the corner of his eye that Lucy had done the same with her own, 'Can't I have a gun? Aaron whispered leaning forward between the seats; Jack made eye contact with him via the rear-view shaking his head minutely to communicate and reluctantly they did as they were instructed, leaving Shep shut away in the car behind them.

Alan and Elizabeth joined them from the caravan they had clearly not armed themselves leaving everything inside the caravan, 'Riggs, Molby commandeer their vehicles,' another order, *who does she think she is?* Jack kept he thoughts to himself. Two of the armed men at the enormous woman's side, moved toward them leaving her and two others, both of whom continued to train their weapons upon them. she picked up again 'well then... who do we have here?' Her voice drooled with some form of excitement, *she really ought to keep her voice down*, Jack twitched his finger waiting for the right moment he was sure it would come, the way she was shouting off was sure to draw attention from any dead in the area.

None of them spoke instead their silence interrupted by sudden screams coming from the car behind them, Shep had lunged at the man the instant the door opened, viciously sharp teeth mangling his left arm, he fell to the floor rolling upon it screeching in agony as he cradled his ruined arm with the working one, weapon abandoned at his side. *That's one down nice one Shep,* a smirk crossed uncontrollably over Jack's lips, wiped away by the woman's next order.

'KILL THE MUTT!' before any of the remaining men could move Jack and Lucy had drawn their weapons, aiming them at the two remaining armed men, 'RIGGS! GET YOU LAZY ASS BACK OUT HERE!' her voice gave away an audible note of fear as the man appeared at the door of the caravan taking in the scene through heavily hooded eyes, raising his gun.

He re-joined his team making three to their two all training their guns on Jack and Lucy. 'So, we're going to up a fight are we?' The woman laughed flinging her head back in delight, she removed her helmet revealing a very bulldog like face, a pig-like nose did little to draw the attention from her awful eyebrows, it reminded Jack of the logo of a fast food franchise that went bust not long ago, he held back the urge to burst into laughter, *now is not the time* 'Oh... *where* are my manners, I should at least give you the luxury of knowing who we are before I *allow* my men to kill you,' she paused a smile clearly visible in the stream of light, showing off a set of rotten teeth.

'I...' an over-the-top gesture, hand on heart as though she were performing in a play 'am Dendre Falls leader of the blood-hunters, our purpose is to cleanse the world of weaklings... like you,' she finished a bigger smile spreading across her face, revealing more stained teeth, giving the impression of an evil toad.

'Kill them,' turning away carelessly flinging a pudgy hand over her shoulder *'starting* with the old ones,' the guns began to fire Jack squeezed the trigger flinging himself towards Alan and Elizabeth, caught by surprise that his bullets found two of their assailants the fell to the floor dead the third Riggs was still standing his gun lowered dark eyes wide in horror staring at them, he held his hand up gesturing his surrender.

He dropped his gun to the floor the sound forced Dendre to turn around screaming with anger she pulled a gun from one of the downed blood-hunter's bodies, she shot Riggs between the eyes point blank, she turned aiming the gun at Jack her greedy little eyes stared down the sights, but Lucy was too fast, she pulled the trigger and her bullet found its target, it lodged itself in Dendre's neck sending blood spurting, her words lost in a gurgle of blood as she fell the weapon in her hand fired one last shot aimlessly in their direction.

He hadn't seen the bullet escape the nozzle nor where it went all he knew was that it *hadn't* hit him, the blood-hunters were all dead; all except one, Molby was still on the floor clutching his useless arm.

'JACK... LIZZIE... NO PLEASE NO...' Alan's voice was hysterical Jack turned to face him, his heart sinking instantly when he saw what had caused Alan's sudden outbursts. He rushed to help the old man, who had fallen to his knees clutching his wife in his arms, blood blossomed across her chest her breathing was weak and her skin had lost all colour, she had been shot.

Tears in Alan's eyes slowly flowed down his cheeks and into his grey whiskery beard, holding his wife's hand as her breathing slowed, he began to rock her, Jack could here he was humming.

For a second time that day Jack felt helpless he had no idea what he should do, he couldn't let Lizzie die not so soon after Brad he dropped down next to them he had no clue what to do, but every effort they made was useless her breathing growing steadily weaker. It built up inside him a lump rising painfully from his chest he tried to swallow it back but it was too strong, he could feel its pressure behind his eyes forcing tears out and then he relented a heaving sob spilled from him, the agony he felt once again he was faced with someone who he had cared about was about to die, and he was powerless to stop it.

'GUYS WE GOT COMPANY, WE NEED TO MOVE!' Aaron appeared at Jack's shoulder his face extremely pale, Gunshots Lucy had begun shooting, Shamblers had begun pushing their way past the van and had already begun feasting on the remains of the blood-hunters lifeless bodies.

Helping Alan they moved Lizzie into the caravan and ran back to the car, Molby still on the floor nursing his arm, Jack pulled him up and threw him into the backseat, where he was joined by Aaron and Shep who growled menacingly at him.

'Shep, no we can't leave him here we gotta move,' Jack swallowed trying to force his heart back down to its rightful, he could feel the overwhelming grief still hammering to be let out, swallowing as hard as he could at the lump it caused in his throat; the Shamblers had pressed in on them as he pulled the driver's door open, Lucy was in the passenger seat firing out of the window at the creatures bearing down on them,

Apologising Jack jammed his finger on the automatic windows forcing Lucy to stop shooting.

Both vehicles roared into life in unison and Jack watched as the caravan turned to the left heading down an empty side street he went to follow when the engine stalled, when hands began slapping at the windows trying to smash their way into the motionless car.

Shep began to cower barking feebly at the monsters as they banged on the reinforced glass trying to get to them, his hackles were raised, tail tucked away between his hind legs.

Molby was too preoccupied with his arm to even respond to what was going on, the sleeve of his jacket stained red, Jack looked to Lucy who returned the same horrified look he knew was on his own face, even now at the completely wrong moment he couldn't help but appreciate her beauty, he felt himself blush at the thought and turned his attention to the key trying to restart the engine once more.

Don't fail me now! He twisted the keys and the engine spluttered into life, he gripped the wheel, readying their getaway, but it was too late they were surrounded.

 Andrew 11

A shadow crept over his shoulder as he stared at the gravel before him, Andrew's heart dropped he wasn't ready to *die!* He embraced himself and the inevitable end with it, closing his eyes tight; his eyes stung as the sadness poured over his body when a familiar voice boomed over him.

'Hey boy, I'm not going to *hurt* you... Andrew... Wasn't it? But wait you prefer Andy' His eyes snapped open turning to the man who was stood behind him, Peter Aldridge the tall - yet slightly dishevelled, -owner of the Alder-Company building, the man who was in charge of everything that went on below, he even chose Andrew personally over hundreds of other applicants to assist him with a top-secret game release, 'The Camden Vanishing.'

There was a broad smile spread across his face, not an expression of happiness but one of relief, he was wearing the same suit he always wore, but its usual neat manner, was gone he had clearly been through the mill and his appearance echoed that.

Andy pulled himself to his feet and looked at the man in front of him his suit was torn in places as though some one had grabbed at him and Andy couldn't help thinking was it either someone begging for help or a zombie trying to grab him for other purposes, noticing other that Aldridge was completely unscathed, he was a mess but unharmed.

'Mr Aldridge did *anyone* else make it?' Andrew asked looking across the bare rooftop, Aldridge's smile faltered, a grimace of obvious remorse surfacing in its place.

'I'm afraid not, to be completely honest I actually thought it was just me...' a shake of the head 'but please Andy there's no need for formalities now call me Peter,' he pulled off the remains of his suit jacket and threw it to one side, 'it's been stupidly hot up here and the only way down is where you just came from and I'm guessing that, that wasn't a leisurely trip into town either?' he said looking back at the thick black plume of smoke still billowing out of the lift's escape hatch; he seemed unusually calm about it and Andrew was having a difficult time figuring out just how reliable he was, one second he seemed like a saint, next... well Andy thought he seemed a little spoilt and a tiny bit lazy.

Andrew was certain however there had to be another way down, even if it wasn't a way that was usually considered.

They *couldn't* be stuck up here, could they? He moved to the edges of the roof looking down each side in turn, biting at his lip ring something he always did when concentrating, on the south side there was a fire escape on one side of the building but lurking here and there on the balconies were more blundering shapes, he did not expect to see one on the top clawing helplessly up to where Andy had leaned over, only a ladder stood between them.

Caught off-guard he flinched away so violently he fell on his backside on the shingle roof once more.

The only other option he noticed was to jump onto the building to the northmost side, only a couple of feet away but the drop... extremely high and if they got it even the smallest bit wrong they would fall to their inevitable death.

'That building's been abandoned for nearly a year now, it'll probably still be empty,' Peter stood over him 'I was considering expanding over to it, making the company bigger ya know, branch out into more fields like social media and television,' bewildered Andrew looked up at him, the man clearly had no clue, what Andy was thinking.

'Well... I was actually thinking we jump across and make our way down to the ground level,' the idea took Peter by surprise and he looked down the gap to the alley below, then back at Andy a look of uncertainty written in the lines of his face.

'W-what if we misjudge it? I mean... it's an awful long way down.' He stammered but before he had finished the boy was on the ledge ready to jump, 'Andrew stop! you'll fall!' before the words made any impact Andy had sprung forward, landing lightly on the roof opposite, ending up much further from the side than he thought he would; impressed with himself, he quickly turned back to the taller building where Peter was stood with his mouth wide.

'Well? what're you waiting for?' Andrew yelled across to him, 'it's easy just do what I did!' Peter pulled himself up onto the ledge his slightly older frame silhouetted against the sun, he wobbled dramatically, throwing his arms out to steady himself, like a strangely comical bird.

His face was white, and Andy smirked as it twitched with a cocktail of the internal struggle that was clearly going on in the man's head. 'Come on Pete! It's such a small gap you can step across!' the heckle was met but a stony glance as Peter released a deep breath and threw his body forward with clumsy grace. landing awkwardly on the soft roof opposite.

He laughed excitedly, his hands frantically searched his body as if to make sure all of his body had managed to make the leap 'I've never *felt* so alive!' he laughed again 'probably not the best term of phrase… current circumstance an all,' he continued to chuckle like a mad man.

Andrew shook his head, it may not be the best thing to say but he really was beginning to like Peter's odd goofiness they man may have been nearly twice his age but he was most definitely not acting like it, *big old man child* he thought as he turned to the centre of the roof, there was a fire door, set into a small square offset, he assumed must be their way in. He moved closer to it, the wooden door bounced about in the gentle breeze, a gentle *tap, tap* against its frame, they reached it, Andy pulled it open and they disappeared into a windows stairwell.

Their footsteps echoed off of heavily graffitied walls, as the descended one step at a time, keeping in mind that *anything* might be just around each corner, there was light coming from somewhere below illuminating the fascinating artwork, 'What do we do when we reach the bottom?' Peter whispered from behind him, Andrew shrugged he hadn't gotten that far, he didn't even know what they were going to do around the next corner, let alone what could be awaiting them down below.

They approached another door that led to a small corridor they moved into it curiously, many doors stood open revealing empty rooms there was nothing in them except discarded spray cans or overturned furniture, the only sign of life in the entire building looked to be... them.

About halfway down the hall they came across a closed door, a large letter 'A' was sprayed in red with a circle outlining it Andy recognised it as the anarchy symbol, he reached for the handle when Peter stopped him.

'We don't know what could be in there,' he whispered his face white eyes wide, 'maybe we should perhaps *knock* first?' He made a valid point if there was something in there if they knocked they would find out.

Andy raised a hand to knock loudly on the door, there was no answer so he moved his hand back to the handle, 'You know what that symbol represents?' Peter asked as Andy began to pull the handle down.

'It means anarchy right?' opening the door but not taking his eyes off Peter expecting more, *surely that wasn't all he had to offer...*

'That is the gist of it yes, but there's more to it than that, they symbol is actually used in the occult,' *now that's something new...* 'Anarchy came about because of Aleister Crowley, heard of him?' Andy nodded 'He coined the term "Do what thou whilst" do what you want and they – satanists – consider it their "Mantra", fascinating really,' Andy nodded in agreement.

'Now depends on whether whoever tagged the door was just following a trend or...' Andy trailed off.

Stepping into the room he looked away from Peter taking it in properly for the first time, the room itself had an office feel to it, but that was the only normal thing about it, the graffiti from outside the room had not gone so far as to bleed inside the walls were instead plastered with hundreds of photographs, photographs of corpses, their many faces staring blankly back at them.

The bodies in the photos had their throats slit and blood was clearly visible, Andrew noticed they were all female, all naked, each one shared several traits blonde hair, blue eyes, moderately sized breasts. Tearing his eyes away Andy looked around the other components of the room there were tables lined up against the window – which had been covered with newspaper clippings - spread out neatly upon them was an array of knives of varying sizes and shapes, one thing was obvious they had stumbled upon the lair of a serial killer.

Andy moved towards the knives, picking one up he examined the long blade admiring the professional way it bent back on itself to form a hook, as sharp as the blade, he noticed its blade reflected the room behind him something moved, he looked to his right Peter was stood next to him reading the newspaper's pasted to the windows, then the door slammed behind them, forcing him to spin towards it; a hooded figure was blocking their escape a small blade gripped firmly in his hand.

'That does not belong to *you...boy!*' deep and drawling, stepping towards him the blade of the small knife raised upwards menacing, but not as menacing as the blade in Andy's own hand, which he raised mechanically forcing the figure to stop a deep laugh spilled from the hood 'well, well, well... we *are* brave, aren't we!' this time Andy recognised the voice.

'Dad!?' the words had left his mouth before he could prevent them, the killer who had started edging closer again, was struck dumb as the words hit him, *this is absurd how could it be him?* Yet the more pieces he put together the more they fit... they way he always disappeared for no reason for days on end. That police radio in his office. The way he seemed so engrossed in the newspapers in the evenings... that smirk that always appeared on his face whenever he read about specific headlines!

The killer lowered his hood, revealing the unmistakeable silver hair and identifiable eyes, one brown the other... green, just like his.

Gale II

Before Gale could even think to do so himself, Collings had already drawn his gun, fired and already silenced a creeper, Gale pulled his own pistol up, locking his target firmly in his sights, he pulled the trigger, his bullet flew through the air before burying itself into the temple of the dead man's skull watching as it fell, in a split-second he had adjusted his aim firing a second bullet before the first limp body had even settled on the floor, again it hit this time entering through the occipital, and he watched as the second of his kills drop to the dirt.

'This is getting a little... *too* easy,' he heard Collings mutter under his breath, Aurora was still crying, he tried to calm her but she was having none of it, he retrieved her from his jacket and held her in his arms again. The familiar scent of the sewer returned to his nostrils he wrinkled it and watched as the baby in hands arms did the same,

'Collings if think she's just... you know,' he held her up to him and he recoiled holding his nose.

'Friendly fire... My God that's potent she hasn't even been fed yet!' he joked wafting his only arm as he stepped backwards, Gale noticed the stump that was all that was left of his other arms had momentarily twitched as though Collings had forgotten it was gone. Gale lowered Aurora to the floor and that was when something caught his eye, hung in the air above the pile of creepers was a woman, he traced the rope wrapped around her ankle to a tree nearby. 'Think I know what got them so riled!' he whispered pointing at the rope, he handed Aurora to Collings and pulled his blade from his waist, gripping it in his mouth taking care not to cut himself with its sharpened edge, he moved quickly but quietly. Up in the tree he could see her better and without hesitation began cutting at the rope within moments he had hacked through the knot tied to the tree.

The woman fell onto the pile of bodies her arms flying in all directions as she tried helplessly to pull herself out from the gruesome heap, Gale dropped cat-like from the tree, and rushed to help.

Holding out his hand for her to grab he pulled her to her feet, she was splattered with foul blood, and Gale could see she was unhurt, she absent-mindedly dusted herself off realising that she was just spreading the wet fluid more she gave up.

She looked up at the two soldiers who had rescued her then at the bundle in Collings' remaining arm it was moving like something in a horror movie, but it was crying.

'Is that a baby!?' She gasped staring at the squirming rags in the man's arm, the man nodded as he tried to show her but with only one arm it was clearly a very difficult gesture for him to pull off.

'We found in the town over there,' Gale murmured as he took the wriggling baby from his injured comrade, 'Think we need to change her rags too,' he finished his nose wrinkled to the smell.

The woman laughed 'I'm guessing you need help with that? I've had plenty of practice -' she stopped suddenly but the younger soldiers holding the child didn't notice as he handed her to the woman.

'Please... I don't have a clue... Just be careful she's very... well... *new?*' he mumbled the woman chuckled at this too but took Aurora from him and he watched as she removed the soiled rags, she cast them to one side and looked back up at him.

'Do you have any clean nappies or... more rags? And some water if you have any...' She asked Gale who returned a look of uncertainty, then looked to Collings who appeared to shrug – it was difficult to tell now - threw his pack onto the floor rummaging through it with his lone arm his withdrew a clean bandage, and some small rags.

Gale transferred them from him to the woman, he checked his canteen for water but it was empty, 'I'll go get you some more water from the river,' he said and hurried back to the river, he was at its edge when he saw his reflection in the murky water, *the sewer runs into this better not risk it,* looking around for another source he ran further down the river eventually coming to what he assumed was a natural spring the water gurled from an unseen source in a rocky outcropping he filled his canteen and hurried back to where the others were waiting.

Aurora was still bawling and Gale was thankful that she was he had gotten lost on the way back and was able to find them through focusing on her cries, he placed the canteen next to the woman who picked it up, using the water to wet one of the rags, promptly wiping the baby's messy bottom, when she got off as much filth as she could she delicately lifted the baby legs placing the small rag underneath before wrapping it in place with the bandage.

'It's not ideal but it will do for now,' she called when she had finished 'we need to find some proper nappies or something as soon as possible and something for her to drink... formula is best, unless we can find a more natural source,' her request was acknowledged she then continued 'it appears we don't know each other's names I'm

Abigail,' she finished looking at the two men in turn waiting for one of them to answer.

'Ok... well this is Specialist James Collings and I'm Private Alex Gale,' Gale spoke as if reciting a well-rehearsed speech 'you can call us by whichever name you choose, oh... and her name is Aurora,' he ended in a less robotic tone, gesturing towards the baby now dozing in her arms.

'Well Alex... James... thank you for rescuing me, but I think we should get moving, only my friend Danni is out here somewhere and she was being chased last I saw,' Urgency was clear in her voice and in silent agreement they set off, through the darkening woods, it wasn't long before they found themselves under the cover of complete darkness, it was so dark that they couldn't see the trees around them, it was time to stop, so they did.

Collings slumped against a tree Abi sat near him Aurora cradled in her arms, as Gale went off searching for something to make a fire, he clicked on his torch and that was when the screaming started.

It wasn't too far away a frantic terrified scream, reverberating through the darkness almost amplified by the shadows, he sprinted back to their barely assembled campsite he was revealed to see they were ok but the shrieking repeated.

'Its Danni,' Abi's eyes were wide 'We have to help her!' She spoke quietly trying not to wake the sleeping Aurora who was now stirring slightly.

Gale wordlessly signalled to Collings to stay and sprinted off in the direction of the screams, his gun poised ready for another encounter.

 Benjamin II

Ben woke to a dull throbbing on the back of his head, making it feel lighter than normal, *had he been drinking?* he lay still for a moment sobering up in the darkness; he could see a dark outline moving around him darting between the openings in the old barn walls.

He forced himself into a sitting position his head spinning as he did so, dizziness set in on him, so he shut his eyes to settle the uncomfortable feeling, he opened them in time to see soft light filter for a moment through the open hay door, but it was quickly dispersed as the door was shut again, the silhouette turned away from it and dropped down next to him.

'In a wee pickle are we not!' he whispered an accent clearly noticeable as he leaned in slightly revealing his face faintly in the limited lighting, he wore an eye patch over his left eye and Ben could make out a long shaggy reddish beard dropping down from an otherwise bald head 'Paddy Flynn is me name,' he added extending his hand out for Ben to take, he looked at it hesitantly the man must've noticed as he spoke again 'ah yeh sorry fer knocking yer out with me shovel laddy,' the accent made his voice sound jovial almost calming.

'Benjamin Towe,' Ben took the extended hand and shook it.

The strange man smiled before he continued 'sorry 'bout me not askin' yer if ah kin use yer barn only ah bin running from they critters fer a few days now,' he whispered nodding his head in the direction of the closed hay door.

Ben had completely forgotten about the strange people outside and his mind went straight to his father, Mary and Greg were they safe?

He jumped to his feet, the pain in his head caused him to sway slightly, but he ignored it and moved to the raised door, pushing it open just a crack he peered through, the sun was high in the sky bathing the fields below in its golden rays, the large farmhouse was visible from here, it stood high and proud on the crest of a hill overlooking the entire estate.

He saw littering the fields between where he was and his family were supposedly hiding, were several of the strange creatures wandering aimlessly around the open land.

The old pickup stood in front of the house he had attached a new wheel the other day and the tank was full, if they were going to survive they had to leave the farm, he closed the door again and turned to the one-eyed man.

'So, Paddy was it? What do you know about these, creatures?' He asked sitting back down on the wooden hayloft floor.

'Ah was waiting fer yer to ask, all Ah know is that ye have to smash in they 'eds, otherwise they keep gitting oop,' he answered 'oh and don't git bit, cause that's how ye become one' he added.

Ben remembered where the thing bit him leaving only a bruise on his arm 'what bit like this?' He raised his arm for the man to look at but it was too dark to make anything out, 'come over to the light,' he added.

He pushed the hay door open the tiniest bit again enough to illuminate the mark on his arm, the bald man examined it with his one eye he shook his head 'ye must be the luckiest I've seen I think it's only when they break ye skin,' he dropped Ben's arm with a smile on his whiskered face.

A sound returned Ben's focus back out of the door, a gunshot, his father was stood in the back of the pickup truck with his shotgun and he could see Greg and Mary running round it to get into the cabin they were making a run for it! He watched as his father shot at one of the creatures the shot hit it in the torso knocking it from its feet, it still picked itself back up a large hole clearly visible through its chest even from this distance Ben could make out the fear lining his father's face an expression he had *never* seen cross it before now.

He had to get to them before they left him alone to die he ran to the top on the ladder Michael on his heels 'what're doing?' He shouted descending the ladder after Ben, who looked left and right he looked for something to use as a weapon something sharp.

He remembered the axe he used to break the lock he had left up on the hay loft, he clambered back up despite Paddy's calls of losing his marbles, grabbing the axe he climbed back down jumping from the ladder when he was low enough. Luckily the others would have to drive past the barn to reach the road maybe if he got out in time he would meet them as they passed.

He kicked at the door it opened onto the yard where at least ten creatures stood all of a sudden the began ambling towards them Paddy had his shovel raised ready when a gunshot sounded and three of them collapsed, the rumble of the engine drew near more gunshots fired leaving only one standing Paddy hit it with his sharpened shovel, cleaving it's head in half Ben grasped the axe firmly expecting it to once more rise from the dead, but it remained on the floor second life used up and gone. The pickup skidded to a stop allowing them to join Felix in the flatbed.

Banging on the top to tell Greg they were all aboard they sped on up the dirt track past more of the creatures Felix's shotgun shouting as the old farmer stood firing at many as he could, the pickup hit a large pothole in the road and the old man was sent tumbling over the truck's side dropping his shotgun in the truck, unknowing the truck trundled on, leaving Felix on his own.

'GREG, FOR THE LOVE OF GOD STOP... STOP!' Ben started yelling pounding on the window for Greg to notice, he saw Felix pick himself up and begin running from more of the creatures, but he was noticeably slowing.

Ben threw himself out of the flatbed and ran to help his father axe in hand Paddy in his tail with his shovel ready, the old man had tripped and they were feet away, he saw the last words he wanted to see form on his father's lips 'leave me!' His vision blurred as the dead caught up with the old farmer, a burning numbness flooded through him as he watched on in horror.

Paddy pulled him back in the direction of their vehicle but couldn't move he couldn't leave the man that had cared for him his entire life to die not like *this!* Not without saying goodbye! He watched as his father disappeared amidst a crowd of bodies his hand drenched in his own blood still visible above the pile of bodies, it was clawing weakly against the mass surrounding him as though waving a sad farewell and he watched as it dropped limply disappearing into their midst.

He allowed Paddy to pull him away at last clambering back into the flat-bed, Paddy banged on the roof to tell Greg to move, Ben dropped to his knees 'dad… I'm so sorry…' and the truck rumbled back into motion.

Peering back to where he had last seen their father and the mass growing smaller began to disperse, a sudden ripple of disquiet erupted over him his father was gone and there was no getting him back.

'Its ok ter cry lad,' Paddy consoled as Ben tried to control the emotional he has shunned for so long, shunned to make his father proud. Taking Paddy's advice, he let out a long sorrowful below causing Mary to look back.

She placed her hand on Greg's shoulder for him to stop, the road was clear and there was no sign of any of those creatures, so Greg did as he was told.

She climbed at of the cabin with as much grace as her seven-month bump would permit and her face appeared over the edge of the truck, 'Where's Dad she asked, tears welling in her eye, the conclusion already upon her before either of the men could tell her.

Grayson jumped from the cab as well and was at Mary's shoulder when he realised she was crying, 'Where's mister Towe?' his underdeveloped mind needing more information than Mary's had.

'I'm sorry but he's gone lad,' Paddy prompted sympathetically but the words were still lost on the stable boy, 'gone... where?'

'Greg... he's... he's...' Mary was unable to finish as a wave of fresh tears consumed her, her voice cracked and she collapsed at his feet sobbing uncontrollably.

'Greg he's... dead,' Ben wailed, and that was when it hit him Ben's voice had lost all hint of derision they was pity in it, a caring note trying to make him understand.

He fell to his knees next to Mary holding her tightly as tears trickled gently down his cheeks.

'It... be... ok... miss Mary... I got you,' he whispered dully through her thick curls of hair, as he hugged her.

The man who had down so much for him since he had been orphaned so many years ago, taking him in fed a watered him and gave him a bed to sleep in, appeared over the hill behind them, his life left behind as his body continued to walk.

 Alice II

Alice held metal pipe out as the wall of living dead approached striking at anything that came within their reach, needing the speed of her bike to deal any *real* damage but it still spluttered into nothing, when a firm kick suddenly resurrected it as its engine roared back from the dead.

Straight ahead of them was a gap and the bike pulled longingly towards it, sending any of the smothering crowd flying in all directions, they sped off through countless more just looking for somewhere to go.

'You're not looking for another flaming ice cream truck are you?' Harrito screamed over the roar of the engine, Alice shook her head scouting the streets for any sign of something other than the blundering mass of the dead.

They passed many buildings until one caught her eye stood on the drive was a police car, distinguishable by its white body decorated by blue and yellow tattoos, and for once the street was clear, she pulled up alongside the car and propped the bike up.

'This time I'm coming with you, we need something other than an old pipe, they could have guns in there,' she was excited at the prospect of having a different kind of weapon than her faithful but limited bar of metal.

The door to the police station was hanging from its hinges bloody handprints leading their way inside, her pipe raised ready and Harrito on her heels they entered, the building was dark and *almost* silent there was a scratching noise of feet scuffing on a concrete floor to their right, they moved towards it.

They found themselves in the cell room where metal bars would separate the felons from the officers, three of the four cells were empty the last one was not, as they passed a hand reached out but not for attention, its owner another reanimated body pressing itself keenly against the cold metal bars, feet scuffing on discarded papers and loose stones on the concrete beneath them.

Ignoring him Alice looked ahead for an armoury or an evidence lockup, but none of the doors were labelled, she pushed aside an overturned table, stepping forward her foot kicked something small that jingled merrily as it skidded across the ground, a ring of keys, she stooped down to pick them up, they hung in her hand, tiny little cell keys and a car key hung from a carabiner and more keys to doors leading to rooms unknown.

Swinging the keys around her finger she crossed the room to the closest door, thumbing through the keys testing each suitable one with the door, finally she found one that fit and turned it in the lock opening the door to an empty interrogation room a lone table stood in its centre chairs on either side, disinterested she turned away moving onto the next frame illuminated partially by the sun shining through the wonky blind on the window.

This time it was the first key she tried opening the door into a room filled with filing cabinets, she went to turn away when she saw on the wall a cage at the far end of the room and inside it a *huge* selection of weapons, *'JACKPOT!'* rushing to the cage she dropped the keys in her haste picking them up again she thrust a key into the lock, once again it was the correct one *two in a row but no lottery to bet on…* twisting the key, it clicked to signal it had unlocked, pulling the chain of keys out she handed them to Harrito who stood at her shoulder 'see if the car outside works,' she mumbled 'we're gunna take them all!' her voice was flushed with excitement, as she studied the weapons she saw standard issue pistols, riot shields and even a high quality Smith & Wesson.

There were ammo boxes, everywhere and even Kevlar vests, underneath a bench in the corner were large bags suitable for carrying multiple weapons three in total. She filled them, with as much as she could she even managed to find silencers taking care to bag them just in case.

Finally, packing two hand grenades carefully into the last bag when a shadow loomed over her, Harrito was back and he was wearing a huge smile on his face.

'Is the car good to go?' Alice asked he shook his head the smile on his face growing larger.

'Something better,' he spoke with an air of excitement which Alice welcomed, 'put it this way we can have the new vehicle and your bike with only *one* person driving,' his smile was so big now his glasses rose off of the bridge of his nose.

Curiosity peaked Alice grabbed two of the bags glancing back at the few weapons she had left behind, leaving the third to her companion they walked back to the open door, past the dead man in the cell still grabbing at them.

On the drive stood a large, modified riot van, with a ramp on the back, and a cattle plough attachment fitted firmly to its front bumper, Alice unpropped her bike and rolled it into the back of the van securing it with rachet strap that locked neatly into the floor, dropping the two bags on her back next to it.

'So? What you think?' his smile still forcing his glasses from his nose Harrito passed his bag to her, she pulled out the beautiful silver Smith & Wesson pistol and a box of ammo from it.

'I think it's the best thing yet!' and climbed out onto the street pulling him into a huge hug finally dislodging his glasses fully, he caught them before the hit the floor, flushed by the sudden gesture.

They pulled themselves into the cabin, Harrito behind the wheel, his head just high enough to see over it, Alice chuckled at his enthusiastic yelps, as she loaded her gun spinning the barrel when she was done.

She aimed the weapon out of her window and pretended to shoot something, imaging the head exploding dramatically as the bullet ripped through it, she withdrew it stared lovingly at her new toy, an enormous grin pulled her lips from a set of near perfect teeth she leant back in her seat as the engine started; they began moving Harrito still giggling maniacally, *my little psycho,* she thought as he ploughed through the dead on the streets laughing louder each time he mowed one down, 'the plough works!' his face was covered in a weird sense of glee.

His glee only surfaced briefly as he turned onto a highway they had travelled along it for coming up thirty minutes when they were forced to stop. Ahead of them the road was filled with cars blocking their way and lurking between the metal wrecks were more walking corpses their skin decaying in the midday sun.

Alan III

Alan glanced at the wing mirror as he hurtled through the harbour town's empty streets, Jack's little car was not visible in it, had they fallen behind? His mind turned to his wife he was still bleeding heavily on their bed that sat at the back of the caravan.

He had to find his way out of the town somewhere he could stop and tens to his wife's wound, the buildings on both sides dropped suddenly out of view and were soon they were barely visible in the distance, the road he was on was open and clear, he recognised it as the same road they buried his son.

He pulled up by a tree with his name carved onto it, moving quickly he knelt next to his wife, her breathing was very weak and there was a slight gurgle at the back of her throat.

'Lizzie, my dear you're going to be ok I'm here,' he whispered through the unbearable wave of grief that swept over him.

'Al... Brad... I Can... see... our... so-,' her voice cracked with the effort, her eyes hardly open but there was a smile on her lips and a single tear rolled down her cheek, 'Don't... worry... about... me... I... love... you... so...' each word came with an effort that Alan wished she could just finished she did not finished what she was about to say, he watched as she struggled to fight away the shadow of death that was taking her from him, but as her breathing slowed it suddenly stopped, her body collapsing as all life – seventy-four years of it - escaped her in an instant and all too final way.

The tears came and Alan could do nothing to stop them, his whole family had gone in the space of a day, not taken from him naturally either, his body shook with the crushing emotion as he held his wife's limp body into one last embrace.

Tears flooding into his beard and finding their way to the floor gradually through the tangled mess of hair, he rocked her backwards and forwards, humming the song that came to him early, it was their song, he remembered as it played throughout their lives; from the days they were young enough to still dance through the night alone in their house, the day Brad had been born, their wedding day and the day they met, the memories flooded through his brain, bringing with it happier times and he cursed the inability to be happy! He cursed the waves of horrible loss that filled him, as the woman he had been married to and loved for the eternity of fifty-two years lay in his arms as he embraced her, her arms hanging limp and unable to return any form of consolation.

He had been crying for a long time and the night had begun to press in he was tired, he was alone and he was vulnerable; soon he was asleep, his wife's lifeless body lying across him peacefully.

When he awoke the sun had begun to rise beyond the windscreen, peering through the trees lining the road, but he was not alone, pounding on the windscreen were more of the creatures that had started all this! the whole caravan surrounded by the hateful, pitiful things trying to force their way in.

The doors locked and he knew they would not find a way inside, so he sat there his wife still sprawled over him. He looked upon every bloodied face snapping at him through the thick glass, he remembered the guns they had taken from the cabin hidden away beneath the bed and he could feel them pressing tantalisingly against his leg.

He pulled the closest one out checking the chamber for a cartridge, cocked it, he placed the nuzzle of the gun under his chin he positioned his finger on the trigger hovering over it, he looked down upon Elizabeth's face one last time, there memories returning how when he first laid eye upon her and in that instant he *knew* they were to marry, but it shouldn't have ended like this! *we will be together soon* he told her silently, his eyes streaming with sorrow he swallowed *all three of us,* a single gunshot echoed out around him.

Afterthought

Hey if you're reading this whichever way you chose eBook, paperback or may a hardback? Once you finished wiping away the tear for our lost companions I would like to remind you, there will be a sequel and also I'd like to first apologise that it has taken a long time! And secondly thank you personally for choosing Zombie-Nexus!

I started writing this eight years ago and well if I'm entirely honest never thought it would come to anything and as I sit here typing away at this passage of text, I am feeling a strange array of emotions.

I won't divulge on all of them and simply highlight the made three.

Excitement: A PAPERBACK VERSION!

Sadness: I just reread it and that ending really... choked... me up.

Fear: I hoped you liked it, I'm certain you have but there's no cure for that niggling doubt but I enjoyed it so why wouldn't you.

I want to sign off by saying the compulsory thankyous, to my family Mum, Dad, Shaun, Elaine, Diana, Laura and Nick, as my brothers and sisters you really mean a lot to me and I used aspects of you for most of my characters – I hope you didn't mind – everyday has been a struggle finding exactly what it is I am good at and no matter what passion I have followed you have all been their to support and encourage me and I am extremely appreciative of that I love you all.

Now I can't go about thanking my family without sending a thankyou to everyone else that I consider family, Helena, Abby, Joly as the light of Shaun's world I may not see you much but again I miss you and wish in the future to see much more of you.

Jason, Alana, Maddox, Eire and Edward again on the beck and call of dear Elaine I don't see you as much as I'd like to but you are forever on my mind.

Team Diana - Teagan, Thia and Willow and see you more but still not enough you all have quirks and personalities, which are just so inspirational to me!

And lastly on the family front Simon and Karl, you are the most recent chosen family member and you make Laura so happy, you may not be related in blood but you most certainly are family! I am happy to call you my brother and nephew respectively.

Now onto the oddities I call friends starting with Scott and Lou you two genuinely are the most selfless people I know, its strange how we barely seemed to know each other but *always* had each other's backs and now we know one another so well that we still got each other's back, there is no one I'd rather turn to when I want to talk about things that I've been through and Scott I know when you're reading this, you will most likely say something along the lines of 'Hey... Hey... Lou. Our names are in a book.'

To which Lou will probably say 'I know I've read it,' and leave the conversation at that.

To Darrell and Cliff for twins you are so different yet the same at the same time, you are my oldest friends and no matter what you are always there when I need you even if you are busy you still make time for me, I know we had our differences but I'm glad you both are there and whenever you need me I will always return the favour.

There are many other people I would like to thank personally but unfortunately if I did this book would be thousands of pages long and if you're still here with me now and you have affected my life in any way good or bad just know I'm thankful for the impact you have had in my life because I wouldn't be where I am now without your help!

And very last thank you Daisy you are the one I want to thank most be you snuggled up to me and giving me kisses and hugs, I am forever grateful for your presence in my life you are always happy to see me and only ever hold a grudge with me if I don't feed you, even then its never on your mind long and you are so willing to forgive me...

guys Daisy is my dog as I sit here writing this she is staring at me, this kind of love is what life is living for!

About the Author.

S. Fairbrass started writing when he was in school but only really hit his stride when he turned 21 the book you hold in your hands is the product of that and although at the time of this book's publication there are no other release's. He has written several other stories.

He is not the owner of any writing awards, he does not intend to make money for his works just tell a story that grips the reader from page one and keep you hungry for more, the first copies printed of this book were donated to charity shops the encourage further financial donations to the shops themselves, paid for by himself and given away for free and it had always been his intention to do this and has vowed to do the same with every book that is to come.

Printed in Great Britain
by Amazon

15698007R00171